BEYOND THE PINES

BEYOND THE PINES

Mark Raymond

First Edition

This is a work of fiction. Names, characters, places, and incidents either are the product of the author's imagination or are used fictitiously. Any resemblance to actual persons, living or dead, events, or locales is entirely coincidental.

ISBN 979-8-9902289-2-4 (e-book),
ISBN 979-8-9902289-3-1 (paperback)

Manufactured in the United States of America

Dedicated to my wife, Jennifer,

for her endless patience, counsel, and love

1

Jake stood perfectly still. Eyes closed, his breathing deep and controlled as he tried to absorb all the peace that his surroundings provided. He inhaled the fresh mountain air. He felt the softness of the needle bed covering the hard earth. He listened intently to the rhythmic ebb and flow of branches swaying and rubbing as the breeze made its way up the mountain, mixing the smells of earth and pine in Jake's nostrils.

Jake was in his temple of solace. The place where he came to process, to work through the sequence of events that framed his young life. Jake was again in the pine grove.

His mind drifted to the time that his father had introduced him to the grove. Jake remembered his instant awe of the tall fortress of mighty pine trees. He could still recall the feeling of power that the grove held for him over the rest of the forest, the invisible walls surrounding the area, insulating it from the rest of the world. Jake concentrated on how the sound of the nearby river and birds calling to each other with warnings and beckons all disappeared as soon as he stepped on the soft pine straw that carpeted the expanse of the grove. He could still see in his mind's eye the powerful canopy of trees as he looked up, allowing just peeks of light to filter from the sunny blue sky to the earth below, casting a calming aura throughout the space.

"It's really something, isn't it Jakey?" Jake could still hear his father ask.

In the present, Jake subconsciously lowered his gaze from the sky as he did back then to meet his father's. He could still hear himself uttering his simple reply. *'It's amazing, dad'*, he recalled saying with eyes wide with awe.

Jake was now staring blankly into the grove. It had been years since his father had introduced him to the majestic space. Sadly, he knew what was coming next, as his mind jumped from the warmth of the grove to the coldness of the beige linoleum tiled floor. His mind no longer allowed him to enjoy the happy memory any longer, now replaced with memories of the long hallway. The muted glow of soft sunlight now replaced with harsh, sterile fluorescent lighting. The quiet stillness evicted by a myriad of mechanical beeps and motors, monitoring vitals and powering breathing machines. Jake's next memory was of standing outside the hospital room, feeling the final second of nervousness and apprehension of what he would see on the other side of the hospital room door.

Jake was now pacing in the grove. Trying to will the painful memories to fade quickly, substituting them with those of better times. He stopped pacing and squatted against one of the pine trees, knees held tightly to his chest. He forced a different memory to the forefront of his mind. This time Jake was waving his hand up and down in the wind, his arm extended out the window of his father's truck. He and his father were yet again making their way to help a friend. Jake felt the cool breeze wash the heat of the sun from his face as he stared at the bright blue sky above the canopies of trees along the wooded road.

Jake always enjoyed winding through the roads of Pine Grove, Vermont, the village that he had called home all his life. The small hamlet, nestled between Mount Smith to the east and Squire Lake to the west, had been bustling with textile industry in its day. It now relied on business from outdoorsy folk and tourists enjoying the mountain and the lake, and harkened back to a simpler time before Y2K and 9-11, both invasive events still fresh in everyone's minds. The woods surrounding the town had the best that the outdoors had to offer, filled with thick, lush fields bursting with wildflowers in the summer, oaks and maples that provide nature's best color show in the fall, and large groves of majestic pine trees. To Jake, his grove was the largest and grandest.

"Almost there, Jakey," Jake recalled his father saying to him with a large, warm smile on his face, "we'll see what kind of crazy stuff Red has for us this time." Jake loved these outings with his father, James Cleary. His father, Irish by heritage, was a hard worker who loved the church that he maintained and cleaned as much as he loved his own home. James adored Jake and Mary, his wife and Jake's mother, and did his best to ensure his family had a simple, happy life. While Jake had his father's red hair and chiseled chin, he was thankful to get height from his mother's side of the family.

Whether it be moving a piece of furniture for an older parishioner from their church or repairing the broken Victrola record player at the local historical society, James was always helping someone. Jake relished the opportunity to tag along, even as a small boy. "Always take care of the people you love, and those that can't take care of themselves," was a mantra of his father, and Jake could now hear his father speak these words as clearly in his mind as if his father was standing next to him.

But Jake knew that he wasn't. His trauma took over once again, and Jake was back in the hospital. He could smell the mixed aroma of antiseptic, chemical, and other odors that he was not familiar with and only experienced at the hospital. Jake followed after his mother, Mary, as she entered the room. He recalled immediately feeling panicked seeing his father laying in the bed. He rarely saw his father being still, even throughout the treatments, but his father lay motionless on the hospital bed, the lights dimmed, the numerous machines surrounding him attached to his body through tubes and wires.

His mother brought him to say his final goodbye, and Jake had no idea how to do so.

Jake rose abruptly from his crouch in the grove and could feel the rough bark of the tree tear at his back. "No!" he shouted out loud. "When is this going to stop?!" he cried in anger to the empty grove. Jake began to walk through the pine trees. He wiped the tears that had formed from his cheeks and eyes. He shook his head sharply to shake the previous image out of his mind and make himself shift focus back to the good memories.

Jake's memory now recalled the crunch of the gravel as his father turned onto the worn road that led to their destination and meetup with Red. Jake peered up at the sign arching over the road at the entrance to Camp Megeso, the Boy Scout camp covering many acres just outside of town and adjacent to Squire Lake.

"Gonna help the scouts today, Jakey," he could hear his father declare.

They stopped at one of the cabins and a man about his father's age wearing dark blue work pants, a flannel shirt with the sleeves rolled up his forearms, and a worn ball cap set back on his head came to meet them.

"Took your time again, I see," the man said.

"Now c'mon Red, you're already gonna start harassing us? We haven't even started," James replied, smiling with a smirk and a wink towards Jake.

"Just setting the tone is all. Want to make sure Jake here knows who's in charge," Red replied.

"Oh, he knows, but his mother isn't here, so I guess we'll both just have to settle on you," James jabbed back.

Jake remembered laughing at the two men. As far as Jake could tell, Red was his father's best friend. Although he had never seen the two men hang out socially, they regularly helped each other fixing one thing or another. Between his father's custodial and upkeep work at the Methodist church in town, and Red's maintenance role at the scout camp the men had plenty of projects.

"What's so funny?" his father asked.

"You two. Are you two long lost brothers or something?"

The two men looked at each other.

"This guy…related to us?" his father responded first, "with that mug? C'mon Jakey, not on his best day. Why do you think that they hide him all the way out here at this camp?"

Red snorted, taking his turn to respond, "In his dreams that he might share my bloodline. Wouldn't have to wear lifts in his shoes if that was the case. Go home and thank your mother that she was able to get you some height, Jake, so that you can ride the big boy rides at the carnival like I can."

In the grove Jake had stopped pacing now, calming down and slowing his breathing as he remembered the three of them laughing at this exchange before heading off to start working. He opened his eyes to find himself at the edge of the grove where he could make out Squire Lake in the distance.

His memories shifted again to days that he and his father would fish for walleye on Squire Lake. They would troll with spinner rigs for hours in the warm spring sunshine in his father's blue fishing boat, Old Smokey, nicknamed for the plentiful white cloud of burnt oil that never failed to appear as the motor was being started. It was on this lake on one of their fishing trips that James told Jake of his diagnosis.

Pancreatic cancer.

Jake now held his arms tightly across his stomach as he recalled the shock as his father explained his condition. "It ain't good Jakey, I'm not gonna beat around the bush, but you know that your father's a fighter, and I'm gonna fight this thing with everything I got." Jake's mind then flooded with images. His father hooked to IVs. The patches of his hair, gone. The scars from his failed surgery. And most jarring for Jake, his father's frail frame as he tapped all his body's strength to fight the terrible invader.

He also had flashes of his mother crying silently at the kitchen table, the same table where they shared their meals as a family for so many years. He could still smell the bread his mother would bake for the family, served with her homemade Irish stew, especially satisfying on cold Vermont days. He could see the steam rising from the tea mug that his father would put out for his mother for the meal. He could feel his parents' hands in his as they held hands and gave thanks for each other as they sat at that table. He never fully appreciated the love that was always present in his home, shared through gestures more than words, but was now replaced with the anguish and pain that disease had brought into their world.

Jake again focused on that last goodbye with his father. Walking to the edge of the bed. Staring down at the shell of the man that he knew and adored. With all the courage that he could muster, he remembered barely saying 'goodbye Dad' before he fled from the room.

His father died that evening.

"I wanted to say so much more, should have said so much more," he again uttered out loud to the trees, "but I didn't." The tears reappeared, the anger winning this round. Jake turned away from the lake and crashed his way through the grove. The hate and pain fueling his response, oblivious to the elements of the grove.

He felt suffocated. He longed for an escape. He pounded his way to the other side of the grove, moving east this time versus his usual southern path to head home. He was only focused on the fastest way out. He was sprinting now, dodging trees and branches. Jumping on and over rocks. Making his way as fast as he could travel. Trying to outrun his pain.

As he broke through the tree line of the woods he came upon a brown, roughhewn cabin, with a man working on the planked exterior. Jake stopped in his tracks.

"Red?"

The man turned to face him.

"Jake," the man responded with surprise in his voice, "I was hoping you'd be around."

2

The Amoretti family reached the American shore of New York City as part of the Italian diaspora large-scale emigration in the early 1900's. The family split along two paths as it struggled to survive in the new world. One path was music. Natural musicians, John Amoretti and his family formed a band, with John at the helm playing his accordion with a master's touch and a sweet sound that instantly brought listeners back to the warmest of homeland memories. The band enjoyed enough success to stabilize John's side of the family, including recording a few originals and gaining popularity at the Marque Music Club, even securing the coveted weekend sets for 11 weeks straight at one point, a record at the time.

The other half of the Amoretti family chose the less noble path of organized crime. The Amoretti criminal sect was a small group that answered to the larger Mafia. The family's start in organized crime had been a violent one, being used primarily as muscle. After earning respect as effective enforcers, the family furthered their reputation as earners by running the standard mafia rackets including loan sharking, numbers, and protection. The family never talked and never failed to pay up, two attributes critical to their success in the world of organized crime. Even so, occasionally some of the family members flaunted their success in public circles, a very arrogant and dangerous habit.

The RICO Act of 1970 enabled the Federal Government to greatly disrupt organized crime, leading to numerous arrests and convictions through the use of surveillance and recordings. The Amoretti family was no exception to this disruption. Silvio 'The Shine' Amoretti, the head of the family, as well as two of his key compatriots were arrested and convicted on charges of illegal gambling and money laundering, and served 20 years accordingly in federal prison.

Following Silvio's release, he found the organized crime landscape changed. The family was half the size it had been when he went to prison, and only a small fraction of what it had been early in the century. Long gone were the days of being hired muscle or an integral part of the larger Mafia operation. The Commission had effectively neutered the family, leaving them only a small take. It was enough to reward Silvio and the others for staying quiet when they were incarcerated, but not enough for the family to ever grow large again or interfere in the interests of the main families. Knowing no other path, Silvio still needed the family and its 'business' to survive, no matter how limited.

The family based their operations in the backroom of a longstanding delicatessen along one of the neighborhood blocks. The faded, dated facade sharply contrasted the gourmet coffee shop located on one side of the deli, but aligned closely with the closet of a shoe repair shop on the other. As with many city areas, the old neighborhood was in a near continuous state of change and 'urban renewal' making it a challenge for the Amoretti family to maintain its hold and find new business opportunities.

Silvio regularly discussed the family's place in the world with his trusted Consigliere, Archie "The Hammer" Scalero, a lifelong friend from their early days running small tasks for the Mafia captains of some of the larger families.

"We gotta know our place, Arch. We get too big and we'll lose this whole thing of ours. The Commission gave you, me, and Dominic a gift here, we could have lost it all," Silvio would always say, referring to the allowance given by the governing body of the Mafia, consisting of the heads of the five big families of the New York City Mafia. "They kept a piece of the action for us when we got out. Stick with what we know, pay up, keep our eyes open and our mouths shut. We keep the money coming in and keep ourselves out!" referring to prison, or worse, a shallow grave.

"I hear you boss," replied Archie. Silvio and Archie were almost always aligned, including staying away from drug dealing as they both had lost sons to tainted cocaine. "But I gotta say, some of the kids ain't too interested in hearing that," Archie continued, "they're starting to itch. See a lot of money coming into this hood and want a bigger piece. We might have to do something about it, just saying is all."

Silvio thought on this for a minute. He knew who Archie was talking about, his grandson, Sonny "Lackey" Amoretti. Sonny was young and cocky, and foolish as many a young man can be. His head was full of visions of grandeur, no doubt after watching too many episodes of The Sopranos and old gangster movies. He craved the respect of The Commission, instead of being left alone by the larger Mafia family because 'the Amoretti's are harmless, pay up and don't make any issues.' He also wanted the cars, girls, and fun that came with the mobster lifestyle.

Sonny was Silvio's only grandson. Silvio loved him and tried to watch over him after the death of his father, but he recognized his grandson's behavior. He had seen it in the boy's father who fell victim to it, culminating with a needle still stuck in his lifeless body in a crack house two neighborhoods over. Silvio had struggled to rein in Sonny in the past, once barely negotiating a pass for his grandson when he disrespected a made guy in one of the larger families. This had cost the Amoretti's a lot of money and was only granted due to respect for Silvo and his family's past. Even so, a pass under these circumstances was a gift in the world of organized crime.

That gift would not be given again.

Silvio knew that he needed to maintain balance not only for the safety of his grandson, but the safety of the business.

"Go, call in my Grandson," he ordered, "let's see where his mind is on things." Archie did so without question.

3

Jake continued to visit Red. His time was limited between high school, working, and spending time with his mother, but he made the trek through the woods whenever he could. Even on his ratty old bicycle using the shortcut trail that he blazed through the grove, it still took him well over half an hour to make his way to the camp. He rode fast through the streets heading out of the small town, and even faster as he tried to outrun the horse flies that chased him like sentries from the swamps on each side of the road. He tore through the pine forest staying tightly to the worn path to avoid sliding on the long pine needles that could lead to a slip and crash of epic proportions. And like any good teenage boy he always timed his ride to the camp, always trying to beat his previous best effort.

Jake had grown not only to enjoy his time with Red, but to rely on it, although it had taken him a bit of time to figure the older man out. Most days Red drifted between gruff fatherly advice, speeches on the latest political conspiracy theory, and reflections on accomplishments from his past that were no doubt embellished. Jake really didn't mind. He loved that Red would show him how to fix things once, and then send him on his way to try the job on his own. This respect was something that he craved, and also provided a welcome break from the solemn looks that he still received in the years following his father's death.

Red was happy to take Jake under his wing, appreciating the connection to the friend he had lost, and embracing the opportunity to mentor the young man. He continued to teach Jake about basic carpentry, wiring, and plumbing; the difference between using treated and untreated lumber, galvanized hardware versus plain, and how to sweat copper pipe as well as glue PVC. As his trust in and fondness for Jake grew, he took advantage of the archery and rifle ranges at the camp teaching Jake how to shoot and properly respect each type of weapon, and set a Texas rig lure to fish for bass in the pond on the property.

Red's mentorship extended beyond teaching Jake how to fix things. He also felt a responsibility to his friend, James, to mentor his son on the foundations of being a man, or at least his version of it. Red would purposely complain about politicians 'that will pretty much screw over anyone, even their own mothers, to keep their face on camera', with a follow-up like, "See, those people never decided on the type of person that they want to be, they let others do it for them." Another time, as they struggled to remove pitted, rusted flashing from a cabin to replace with new, Red philosophized that, "The true measure of a man is not what he does when people are looking, but what he does when they aren't." He was always dropping sayings about a man having character, and taking care of his family, himself, and his work, but was careful to never directly lecture Jake. He hoped that his ideas and examples were enough without being too obvious. Jake saw right through it, but didn't mind.

Although Jake appreciated and inwardly considered all of Red's lessons, he remained reserved in what he shared with Red. Thoughts and feelings would be revealed only after Jake had formed his own conclusions. Red often found himself navigating many of Jake's decisions in real time. One afternoon as he and Red repaired rotted windowsills in one of the cabins, Jake opened up some about school. It wasn't what Red wanted to hear. "I think that I'm done with school," Jake offered out of the blue.

"What do you mean, done? Ready to graduate? Yeah, I remember that feeling. Young man ready to take on the world," Red responded.

"Nah, I mean done. I think that I'm gonna drop out."

"Now, why you wanna go and do that?" Red replied, stopping what he was doing, and wiping the window glazing from the putty knife.

"I figure, what's the point? I can do what my father did, and am learning about maintenance from you. Seems like enough for me," Jake replied not making eye contact with Red, correctly assuming that he would not be happy with this idea.

Red knew that the kid probably wasn't interested in college since neither of his parents attended and he had never mentioned it. Even so, Red saw this as an invitation from Jake to provide some counsel. "You should finish high school. It would be foolish not to, especially since you're so close."

"I know, but I just don't care about it. I want to do what you do. What does some piece of paper mean to that?"

"You may not get a good setup like your father and I have. It took time to find jobs that let us do our thing without somebody following us around all day to make sure we did it the way they wanted. Besides, your father and I both went to the military after high school. You planning on that?"

"No, I wasn't," Jake said, momentarily stopping to consider the idea.

Red didn't want a single discussion to push him to the military. He knew his own experience, and had decided that was a decision that someone has to make on their own after clear contemplation. Using humor to break the mood, Red added "plus if you don't get that piece of paper, those idiots at school that you can't stand will finish and get theirs, and then they'll be telling you what to do. *Order up Jake!*"

Jake smiled at this and looked at Red, responding, "well, I guess that's true."

Red continued, "And, if for no other reason you should finish for your mother."

Red turned his attention back to removing the rotted sill on the next window. After a pause to let his advice sink in, Red made Jake a proposal. "I'll tell you what, you finish high school and I'll hook you up with a nice graduation gift. And I promise it'll be worth it, trust me."

Jake now looked at Red, his curiosity piqued.

Red, continuing to pry the rotted sill from its place with a screwdriver and his fingers, returned to his usual sarcastic tone, "Now, can we please finish this before it gets dark and I can't see a damn thing?" Jake smiled, picked up a piece of fresh wooden windowsill and started to cut it to length.

*   *   *

Jake was actually intrigued enough by Red's offer to finish high school. The day after graduation Jake came skidding into the camp, tracking down Red.

"Here it is," he said as he offered a piece of folded paper in his hand.

"Here's what?" Red replied.

"Final report card. All C's and one A actually…in Shop," Jake said, proudly.

"I would hope so after the education I've given you," Red replied, smirking. "Alright, c'mon then. I guess you've earned it."

Jake followed Red to a small shed that he was not familiar with. Red switched on the lights and two open bulb fluorescent light fixtures hanging from the ceiling flickered to life. The shed was dusty with a built-in workbench on one side covered with a few loose tools, some cans of old paint, and a few red rags. In the middle of the shed was something covered in a large tarp.

"This has belonged to me for a long time. It's just sitting here collecting dust, so I figured I would put it to good use to get you to finish school. Shouldn't have had to bribe you for Christ's sake, but still. You kept up your part of the bargain, so I'm keeping up mine." Jake knew this was about as close as he would get to an actual compliment from Red.

Red paused, looking at the tarp covered reward. Jake thought he saw the man smile slightly for just a second as if lost in a thought or memory, or maybe even pride or affection for Jake. Red refocused and pulled the tarp. What was beneath instantly caused Jake's eyes to grow wide and jaw to drop. Below the tarp was his gift, a 1981 Yamaha XT500 motorcycle. The bike still had the original red XT and white 500 logo on the silver gas tank with black top, as well as the signature white front fender. It was worn with age but appeared to have recently been tended to. There was a small tear in the black seat, but both turn signals and even a mirror was still in place.

The single cylinder classic, even with clear signs of use on both road and trail, might as well have been new from the showroom floor to Jake.

"So, you can park that bicycle and *graduate* to this…see what I did there?" Red joked, making himself chuckle.

Jake didn't even notice Red's attempt at humor. "Red," Jake said softly, "is this really for me?"

"Yeah, you earned it. You're a good kid, Jake. Take it, I don't ride her anymore. Take her and have some fun. Maybe you can even muster a girlfriend, finally, but I doubt it as soon as she sees the mop." Red always enjoyed making fun of Jake's unruly red hair, nicknaming it 'the mop'. "I cleaned her up, changed the plugs and oil, and started her. She still runs as well as the day I bought her. I always took care of her, and if you do too she'll take care of you for a long time. I'll show you how to change the oil and maintain her, but she is yours now. Here, take this helmet and you damn well better wear it. Your mother is going to be mad enough at me."

Jake stared at the bike, soaking it in. "Thank you Red…thank you…I just never dreamed…," Jake said choking up.

"I know, kid, I know. C'mon, let's get you riding."

After a quick lesson, about an hour of riding around the camp, and a dose of youthful confidence, Jake had complete certainty in his riding ability.

Jake loved to ride the old motorcycle. He especially loved to ride down the back roads at night. He felt total freedom and found it to be his preferred means of escape when the melancholy set in. Many thoughts flashed through Jake's mind as he rode. Quiet dinners with his family, helping his father work in the family's small yard, the aroma that filled the entire house when his mother made banana bread, and the time at the local fair that he and his father rode 'The Vermont Flying Machine' amusement ride over and over until he got sick. Even the act of allowing these happy memories to drift into his consciousness was small progress for Jake in his grieving process. He was eternally thankful to Red for giving him this.

One evening as the sun was just touching the tops of the trees, Jake rode his motorcycle to the cemetery to visit his father's grave for only the second time since his funeral. The first time was shortly after the funeral. At the time Jake figured that visiting the grave was normal behavior and what people did in this situation, but when he arrived Jake couldn't bring himself to get off of his bicycle. He just sat on the path staring at the stone through tear soaked eyes. It only took a few minutes for him to decide to ride off.

This time was a little different. Whether it was the passing of some time, or arriving on the powerful machine, Jake parked his Yamaha on the path and walked to his father's plot. "Hi Dad," he started softly. "I have something to show you." Jake pulled the folded report card from his pocket. "I did it. I graduated." He folded the paper again, crouched, and placed it against the headstone. While crouched he pulled the Swiss army knife that his father had given him and scraped some grass cutting residue from the etched letters on the stone. When finished he rubbed his fingers along his father's name and along the single inscription below the name and date: 'Son, Husband, Father'

Jake exhaled and tried to speak as he thought he should. "I sure do miss you Dad" was all that came out. Jake wasn't as ready for the visit as he had thought. He still wasn't ready to share, to release his anger at the unfairness of his father's death, the injustice done to him and his mother. Jake stood and could feel the anger overtaking the sadness, his usual cycle when he thought of his father's death. Standing, Jake put the knife away while staring down at the headstone.

In a shaky, restrained voice Jake said, "sorry Dad, I'm not there yet...don't know if I ever will be." Jake could feel his body starting to tense. His hatred of that disease and what it cost him was taking over again. Jake suddenly let out a guttural scream. A scream of pain so primitive and raw that he became dizzy from the effort and caused the birds to flee in fear from a nearby tree. The scream echoed into the country air, and Jake found himself holding himself up with his arms, clenching the top of the headstone. As the echo died, Jake stood, turned, and walked back to the motorcycle in one motion.

Jake mounted his mechanical steed, kicked hard to start it, and tore off into the sunset.

4

Sonny swaggered into the back room of the delicatessen like he owned the place. Tall and Italian, he wore a blue polyester polo shirt with all three buttons unbuttoned, black slacks and shoes, and several gold chains with a pendant of the Blessed Mother, the Virgin Mary, hanging from one. He wore a gaudy gold Rolex watch inlaid with a diamond on the face that was actually fake, but Sonny was none the wiser.

He stopped briefly to greet the two senior members of the Amoretti clan besides his grandfather. They were sitting at a small table smoking and talking. One was Archie, who had sent for him. The other was Dominic "Big Dom" Donati, another childhood friend of his grandfather, and clearly second in command. Dominic was barrel chested, well on his way to 300 pounds, and still looked like he could knock anyone out with his giant fist even at his age. Dominic was a traditionalist like Silvio and Archie, and out of respect as well as necessity, lived within the constraints Silvio imposed on the family's business activities.

The two men were finishing a conversation with a family associate, Johnny "the Jeweler" Stints. Johnny specialized in theft, earning his chops stealing jewelry at an early age. At one point as a teenager he managed to steal several high end jewelry pieces from three different stores all in the same afternoon, leading to his nickname "the Jeweler". A pointy nosed, thin man with dark hair slicked back, Johnny was always a little on edge in the presence of the senior gangsters, normally displayed through the tapping of knees or fingers. He was a made man, and a Soldier in Sonny's crew.

"What are you looking at, Jewels?" Sonny shot at Johnny. He stopped his verbal assault short based on the look from Dominic. Quickly changing subjects Sonny asked, "My grandfather in the back?" to which Archie replied, "Yeah, he's ready for you."

Sonny opened the door to the small office in the back of the room. "Grandson!" Silvio said, standing to embrace and kiss Sonny. "How are you?"

"I'm good, Grandfather." Sonny replied. Sonny's father taught Sonny the hierarchy of the family at an early age, and even took Sonny to visit his grandfather in prison. As the years passed, while his grandfather and the others were still in prison, Sonny had become a made guy himself with his own crew.

"And how is your mother? She is well?"

"Si, she is good as well, Grandfather."

"Buona. I look forward to Sunday dinners every week. No one's sauce is better."

"Sonny," his grandfather always used his grandson's name when it was time to talk business, "Your crew is doing a good job, earning, keeping clean. That's good."

Archie had slipped into the office.

"I also hear," Silvio continued before Sonny could interrupt, "that you're not, shall we say, entirely satisfied with things these days."

"Grandfather," Sonny said as a failed attempt to soften the man, "I mean no disrespect, but there is so much money to be made. You, Archie, and Dom have been out for a while now, but we haven't even started to build back to our former selves. I know that I can do that for you."

"I don't need that, Sonny, nor does this family. The Commission was very clear on our place and our

21

responsibilities. Plus, we don't need the heat that comes from the rest of it. We take what is ours and leave the rest to the others," Silvio replied, carefully hinting at the consequences that come with the drug trade and the past deaths. "Look, you have good earners under you, you have nice things and respect in the neighborhood. Don't be greedy and ruin that."

"I understand, this thing of ours is good, but the Amoretti family deserves respect beyond this neighborhood. We deserve to again be heralded in this city. Everyone knowing our names, scratching our backs, greasing our palms. Every restaurant and club open to us whenever we want."

"We don't need any of that. What clubs do you need to be in that you can't get into already, what restaurants are not open to you?"

"Again, Grandfather, no disrespect, but we need to be able to pull bigger jobs because we deserve it. We are earning again, as much as The Commission will let us. They need to see that we can be real earners again and not just some glorified crew. I know that this family can be that again, you just have to let us!" At this point Sonny realized that he might have demanded too much.

"Enough!" Silvio barked as he slammed his open hand on the desk. "I give you much freedom as my grandson, but you will not disrespect me or my decisions as the head of this family," he continued sternly. "What you want brings too much trouble. The answer is 'No'." Silvio paused after making this point to make sure it sunk in. "Do you understand, Sonny?"

After a beat, Sonny replied "Yeah, Silvio, I do."

After the energy of the exchange died down some, the two men stood, embraced, and kissed each other on the cheek.

"I'll see you on Sunday then." Silvio said, with Sonny replying with a simple, "of course," then turning to walk out.

"I don't know, Arch" Silvio mused after Sonny had left the room.

"I do," replied Archie in a matter-of-factly growl, "I'll have Dom keep an eye on him."

5

Red looked up as Jake walked into his utility cabin. "How did it go?" Red asked.

"Just fine." replied Jake putting down the tool bag. "I found the shorted switch in cabin four and replaced it. I replaced the outlet in the bathroom and remounted the towel holder as well when I was there."

"Good," Red replied evenly. "You're starting to get the hang of things around here. Guess even a young dog can learn a trick or two if they get shocked enough times." This was Red's typical way of giving Jake a compliment without expressing too much emotion. "Time for lunch." Red was heating a venison stew in a cast iron pot on the stove.

The two had been working together more regularly in the few years since Jake graduated. When he was able, Jake would stay for the full day, but typically headed home to see his mother for dinner in the evening. While Red still provided mentoring at times, the two typically talked about the work, the weather, or some other shallow topic. Red could sense that Jake still appreciated their time, but more for the camaraderie, environment, and work. Even so, Jake still never spoke about his father.

Through Red, Jake was able to secure a job with the camp helping in the kitchen and cafeteria. Starting with basic serving and cleaning, Jake had been asked to help in the kitchen after the first few weeks. The camp served a fairly basic rotation of burgers, chicken nuggets, and lots and lots of potatoes. While Jake got some time in prep and on the grill, he spent most of his time peeling potatoes and making french fries. He was amazed at how many french fries could be consumed by the several hundred campers that rotated through the camp.

Jake would occasionally break away from working with Red and participate in some of the camp activities. He spent time at the waterfront swimming, canoeing, and fishing, and also enjoyed participating in the evening community gatherings where all of the troops would come together, each taking turns performing a skit or leading the others in a song. These activities allowed Jake to steal back some innocence, a temporary reprieve from the dark feelings that he was still processing from his father's death.

Red didn't mind Jake taking these times, and appreciated the opportunity it gave Jake to behave like a boy a little while longer. He knew the value of that from his own life, and knew how quickly one had to grow up sometimes. For some people, unfortunately, it was almost overnight.

Despite his job, Jake still found time to help Red maintain the camp. Jake found the work a rewarding way to focus his mind, and appreciated not only the prescriptive manner that Red laid out each job, but the independence that Red gave him as he became more proficient. His mind would occasionally begin to wonder if this is how things would have been with his father if he was still alive, but Jake would immediately push those thoughts out of his head. He didn't want to risk the pain that came with allowing himself to grieve properly.

One afternoon Jake showed up at Red's cabin unexpectedly. Red was away, so Jake let himself in to warm some before heading out to look for him. As he looked around trying to figure out where Red might be working, he noticed a small wooden box on a shelf by the window. A round metal emblem with the relief of a bee in fighting mode was inset on the top of the box. Jake hesitated for a second and then opened the box. Inside there were several photos, a patch with the same fighting bee logo as well as the word 'Seabees', and a newspaper clipping. After looking at a few pictures of young, strong men posed in fatigues on heavy construction equipment Jake realized that these were likely pictures of Red in the military.

Jake next slowly unfolded the old newspaper clipping, reading it to himself.

Naval Mobile Construction Battalion Honors Seabees Killed in Action

Five NMCB Seabees perished and ten were wounded in a rocket attack at a Forward Operating Base. The Navy stated that the location of the incident is classified, but that the mission involved advance preparation for defense of civilian personnel under regular attack from enemy aggressors.

Commanding Officer Capt. James Lyle and NMCB Detachment Officer in Charge Lt. Tiayana Sanders saluted each fallen Seabee after placing a wreath in their honor. Lyle shared a detailed memory of the day of the attack, and provided details of the role he and his teammates played in the effort to protect the civilians.

"I consider it a privilege to be able to honor my fallen brothers today," said Lyle. "Each man lived

heroically to the tradition that 'Seabees never quit, never surrender, and never let the enemy break their will to fight.'"

Jake stopped reading the article, looking out the small window at nothing in particular. He blankly stared through the dust in the air illuminated by the sunlight, not noticing the trees moving in the wind, not hearing the robin's call. Instead, he was trying to wrap his mind around the article kept by Red all of these years. Kept in a special box, honored to be one of the few non-essential possessions in the sparse cabin. '*Red knows death too*', Jake thought.

Deeply contemplating, Jake hadn't noticed that Red had come into the cabin while he was reading. "So, what do you think?" asked Red, startling Jake.

"I'm sorry, I shouldn't have opened it...I just...," Jake said while quickly trying to re-fold and replace the letter.

"Don't worry about it," Red reassured him. "Tough stuff, no doubt about that. Was a while ago but still seems like yesterday in some ways," Red philosophized. "I watched five of my brothers, men that I was closer to than anyone on this earth, lose their lives that day. I was able to pull one out, but ended up just holding him as he breathed his last breath looking into my eyes. He tried to mask his fear, but the eyes never lie and only betray our real emotions."

Red continued, "I was a military man. I knew the risks of my business, as did all my fellow Seabees. I tried my best to save them as they would for me. Despite that, there is not a day that goes by when I don't think of them, and while I don't dream of that terrible day often anymore it is still there, and always will be. I tried the usual path of drinking my way past grieving, but it never really worked. Really just prevented me from getting close to anyone. It took a fellow veteran to stop my downward spiral."

"I had to grieve. I had to be angry, guilty, lonely, sad. I had to allow myself to reflect on that day and what happened to those men. I even went back to that location with some of my brothers to try to cleanse, rehashing that day, crying, consoling, holding each other up, and finally realizing that it happened because it happened. Realizing that those men died defending civilians in a situation that had no plan, was nothing we deserved, just was."

"Jake, the loss of your father is something that happened. You did nothing to bring it on. Neither did your mother or father. While it's terrible, I hope that you don't let it define you. I won't tell you what to do, but I am glad that I was able to at least share with you what happened to me and the lessons that I learned."

Jake trembled as he listened to Red, his grip so tight on the newspaper article that he had started to tear the folded paper. He could feel the emotions surrounding his father's death straining to push out of his chest, to come to the surface and be dealt with properly. Jake tried to swallow his emotions again, but they finally surfaced as long breaths followed quickly by tears and sobs. Jake turned to Red and buried his head in the man's chest. Red wrapped his arms around him, more boy at this point than young man, as Jake sobbed.

"It will be ok," Red said, resisting the urge to add more to the end of the sentence.

"It's not fair, Red. Why him? Why did he have to die?" Jake sobbed into the older man's chest. "He was a good man…a good man…he was my father…is my father…," he continued to sob, trailing off as he spoke through choked words.

"I know," Red replied, "there just isn't an easy answer Jake. He was a good man. He, you, your mother, none of you did anything to deserve this. Cancer doesn't play favorites, it just sucks, Jake...it just sucks."

After a minute or two Jake stopped sobbing and pulled back from Red, working hard to regain his composure. He had never been that emotional with anyone and wasn't sure how to act following it.

"Sorry, Red," he said softly.

"Nothing to be sorry about. 'Bout the best thing you could do was that right there," Red responded, "death is hard, it packs a lot into the emotion, best thing is to find ways to let it out so it doesn't consume you." Red continued, "I know that it may not seem like it now, but the sun will continue to rise and each day will bring you closer to healing. I promise that."

"Thanks Red, I really appreciate it...and what you're doing for me letting me hang around," Jake responded.

"What I'm doing for you? You're the free labor on these jobs, you're helping me out," Red joked, trying to lighten the mood.

Jake laughed a little at his joke. "You know, Red, comedy isn't your best skill." They both laughed at the accuracy of the statement.

"Jake, I know that it hurts, and truthfully it will for a while. Just keep going, and remember I'm here to help you through, no matter what."

6

"Cazzo!" Sonny roared. "These guys, they just don't get it, fugget about it.'

Sonny was meeting with Johnny and another associate, Louie Mancini, who was referred to as "Louie Streets" or "Streets", for short by the other mobsters. Louie was an Associate of the family, the lowest rank and not a made guy. Louie's specialty was street crime. He was a decent earner and the newest member of the crew. Sonny seemed to have no interest in recommending Louie for promotion to Soldier, a position that is held by a made guy, a fact that he never seemed to let Louie forget.

Sonny continued his agitated rant, "I love my grandfather, but he and Archie are just holding us back. I know they are all standup guys, even when they went in, but they are just holding me back...holding us back. There is so much more money to be made out there. They just aren't willing to take any risk. I don't get it...no risk, no reward."

The two men could see that Sonny was getting angrier every second. They could sense that he was getting ready to boil over. "Sonny, we're earning," Johnny replied in an effort to calm Sonny down, "everyone's paying up, and the money's consistent and pretty good."

"I don't want just pretty good. Jewels, Streets, go and find us something. We need the Commission to notice us...now!" he commanded. Johnny and Louie stood and left immediately. "And it better be something good!" he added as extra motivation as only he could. Sonny slowly swirled his drink of Cutty & water as he looked after them. As the door was shutting he said aloud to no one in particular, "I love you Silvio, but I'm done waiting."

Outside Johnny and Louie walked a few blocks before they would part ways.

"Man, this is really driving him," Louie said referring to Sonny.

"Yeah, it seems to push up in his mind every so often," Johnny replied, as he pulled the toothpick out of his mouth. "I just hope he doesn't screw up again, not sure we can survive that. Even so, he's the Cappo...he wants a new place, we go find him one."

"Yeah," Louie replied, "about that, I think I got a place. New art gallery where the old frame factory was on the corner. I've been scoping it, and I know that pieces are coming in. Building looks to be secure but not unbeatable, not sure about the gallery. I got a guy who can fence it too. Could be some opportunity there."

"Art?" Johnny considered, "we haven't done that before." Johnny popped the toothpick back into his mouth while he continued to walk and consider the possibilities. "Protection maybe, I could see that, or rob the place, maybe an insurance angle. Not sure anyone else is working that around here. Ever the opportunist, Steets, I'll check it out. Maybe this will scratch Sonny's itch and open up something new for us to exploit...and keep us out of trouble."

7

The brilliant late summer sun warmed Jake's skin. He tilted his head upward and closed his eyes, as if taking in each of the sun's rays. It was the kind of day that lets you know that fall was on the way, but summer hadn't yet given up. Jake breathed in deeply, absorbing all the wonderful smells. His ears captured each of the noises combining them into a single experience. He could sense the bustling of people all around him.

When he had graduated high school he wasn't sure what would come next. This unknowing hadn't bothered him, though. He picked up another job at a store near town, and spent most of his free time with Red at the camp. He had continued to work with Red over the past few years, learning enough that he could identify issues and complete the repairs entirely on his own. They continued to bond, and from Jake's perspective, Red had transitioned from mentor to friend.

Jake had decided to visit the Pine Grove Summer Festival for the first time in years. The Summer Festival consisted of a gathering of local artisans and non-profit booths on the east end of the town green, a few carnival rides and food trucks on the west end, and a small stage for musical acts just in front of the brick town hall. A sidewalk sale complemented the activities on the green, and served as a final boost in sales of active and outdoor wares and equipment before the season change.

The returning memory of the delicious apple pies sold by the Community Church located on the edge of town proved to be Jake's main motivator for returning to the festival. Jake had always loved these pies which were each made from scratch. The dense filling of slices from several apple varieties was perfectly seasoned with extra cinnamon. His family had made regular trips to the farmers market to pick up these special treats, and Jake wanted to share it with Red, so he decided to stop at their booth at the festival.

Before he made his way to the church's booth, he decided to visit his mother. He knew right where to find her on this bright day, where she faithfully worked every Saturday. Jake walked down the few concrete steps and through the doorway into the basement of the Methodist Church. This was the same church his father had worked in, where his parents had met and married, and where Jake had been baptized as a baby. While there were memories of coming to help his father at work, Jake still found some solace in the space. It was filled with fond memories of fellowship, laughter, and his favorite, the church potluck dinners with more food than the diners could eat in three meals.

"Jakey," Jake's mother, Mary, said, looking up from her work and greeting him excitedly as she tended to do. Every Saturday she volunteered in the clothes pantry accepting donations, sorting the items that could be distributed immediately from those that she would take home and mend first, and working with patrons to provide them what they needed. Payment was accepted only if they were able and insistent. Otherwise, she and the other volunteers were doing "the Lord's work," as she liked to say. It was one of the many things about his mother Jake admired.

"Hey Mom," Jake replied, simply. She turned to hug her only son with a gentle and full wrap of her arms.

"I didn't think that I would see you here, what with the fair going on and all," she commented, "what brings you down here?"

"I decided to bring a pie to Red," Jake replied.

"Oh, he is going to love that, going to feel spoiled I bet," she replied with her trademark kind smile.

"Yeah, maybe I'll finally force a smile out of the old grouch," Jake replied snidely, with a smirk on his face.

"Now Jakey, don't talk like that. That man has been good to you, been there for you," Mary lectured lightly, "you be nice."

"Of course, Mom, I'm always nice, you know that," Jake replied as he had to this same lecture many times before.

"You need any help before I head over?" Jake asked.

"No, no, I'm all set here. Just finishing the last box. You go and get your pie for your friend," she replied, dismissing the offer for help with a slight wave of her hand.

"Ok, Mom. I'll see you later," Jake said, "I love you Mom."

"Aw, I love you too Jakey," Mary replied with a smile, "now get going, you don't want them to sell out on you."

Jake left the church and wound his way through the crowd, glancing at popup tents selling wood carvings and hand-crafted silver jewelry as he made his way to the church's booth. Rounding the corner he saw that the line was only a few customers deep. When it was his turn he ordered his pie. The grandmotherly lady waiting on him looked over her glasses perched near the end of her nose and noticed the big smile on his face as she turned to retrieve the pie from the table.

"You're really looking forward to this, I can tell," she commented.

"Yes ma'am, best pie in the world," replied Jake.

"You're not going to steal off and eat this all by yourself, are you? Surely a handsome boy like you has a sweet thing to share it with."

Jake laughed. "Oh, I'm going to share it, but it definitely isn't with a sweet thing." he said, shaking his head slightly and smiling.

"Ok then, dear. Well, I hope that whoever is special enough to deserve a slice."

"They are, for sure," Jake replied, thanking the lady and taking the pie with a smile.

Jake turned to leave heading in the direction of the camp. Jake's smile spread a little wider as the festival feelings continued to buoy his spirit.

Suddenly, he and the other festival attendees heard and felt the large explosion. The terrible sound echoed through the town square as a large ball of smoke rose over the trees in the near distance…exactly in the direction of the camp.

*   *   *

The bright fireball from the explosion could be seen all around, rising above the trees into the clear sky. The type of explosion that shakes the ground. The type of explosion that burns the trees. The type of explosion that occurs when natural gas meets spark. The type of explosion that would change Jake's life…again.

As he sat in the hospital room, Jake could barely keep it together. Red was lying in the hospital bed unconscious. The burns on the back of his neck and left arm weren't even his worst injuries. In addition to the broken arm and three broken ribs, the explosion launched Red through the air resulting in a fractured skull when his head smashed onto the ground, just inches from a rock jutting from the earth.

Losing his sense of smell due to a chemical accident in the Seabees never seemed to really affect Red. He could smell the strongest of spices and aromas, but had to breathe very deeply to do so. Being in no hurry as he entered cabin 8 to perform some repairs, he never noticed the smell of the gas leak in the cabin. As he turned the old, dated switch on, it only took a fraction of a second for the gas to ignite, decimating the cabin and launching Red.

Jake was sitting by Red's bedside well after visiting hours were over. He struggled with the situation and the unfairness of it all. Only recently was he finally able to control his anger at his father's death, but even that was still inconsistent. Jake's mind shifted between numbness and acute thoughts of anger and pain as he processed Red and his injuries. He also felt a strong sense of betrayal. Betrayed by his father, betrayed by a higher power, betrayed by Red, and even betrayed by his beloved woods for bringing him to Red, the first step towards opening up his emotions and vulnerability. All of it represented evil at this moment, an evil that again burned a pit inside him.

"Hey, what are you still doing here?" the nurse who had just entered the room asked Jake. "Visiting hours are over."

"I need to know...how bad is it?" Jake asked, paying no attention to her question.

"Excuse me, I know that this is hard for you, but you really need to speak to his doctor in the morning...during regular visiting hours...to get that information."

"I can't wait for the morning!" Jake snapped, turning to the nurse with a look of masked fury and tears starting to form in his eyes. Calming himself, he continued, "I need to know

now, and I want an honest answer. Can you please help me…please?"

The nurse shifted her weight and subconsciously looked towards the doorway to make sure no one else was nearby. "Ok, but you didn't hear it from me. It's not good. If I had to guess I would say that he has about a week to live, maybe two tops. He has a skull fracture and severe spinal cord injury. Surgery helped, but I have seen it before. I'm sorry, if in fact that is what you really were looking for."

"It was, thank you," Jake mumbled as he turned back to Red. Jake didn't hear the nurse again requesting him to leave. He didn't hear the beeping of the machines, or notice the raindrops now falling on the window. All that he could sense was that feeling of betrayal and rage rising again.

That was it for Jake, the final straw. Something had to give. He was not going to wait around for Red to die. In his mind that would be a burden too big to bear, and he didn't trust himself or his actions to follow.

He had decided. Before Red died on him too it was time to leave.

8

New York City is an organism. Giving life to some and breaking others. Ever changing and evolving to survive. For generations people have turned to the city to save themselves. People have called it escaping, immigrating, 'making it big', all a means of personifying the city as a savior. Jake was no different. His heart and spirit broken, he left his wooded hamlet traveling to the antithesis.

He had recalled the time that his father told him about the city before his family had traveled down to attend a wedding. "Ah Jakey, I'll tell ya, wait till you see where we're going. It's like the other side of the world from what you're used to up here," his father had said. Even at a young age, Jake completely understood his father's perspective as soon as they had arrived for their visit. Now 'the other side of the world' seemed like the perfect place to Jake for an escape.

Jake marveled at the tall buildings and swarming people as he drove the Yamaha into the city proper. He used some of his small savings to rent a room at The Elm Inn. The place was dated and very worn, but provided a cheap, short term rental for Jake as he tried to figure things out. The Elm Inn also had a small fenced in area where he could keep his motorcycle with some level of security, especially after he made sure to purchase a good cable and lock from the local hardware store.

He met all kinds of characters at the cheap hotel. First was an ex-boxer named Joe who used a few too many painkillers to counter the many times he was knocked out. Joe existed in a perpetual conversation with someone else that no one could see, only pausing to extend a hearty 'welcome' to everyone he saw even if it was several times in the same encounter. He met a man named Jaul who always dressed in military fatigues, and seemed to always move with purpose. He only nodded to Jake before making his way to the next part of his 'assignment'. There was also a couple of starving artists, Spider and Trei, who created jewelry from broken glass and other small items discarded as trash in the city streets. These, and a variety of other characters, inspired Jake to either stay in his room or head out into the neighborhood to look for work.

His room had faded gray walls, a threadbare rug, cast iron bed frame that had been painted several times, an antiquated desk, and a worn wooden chest of drawers. At first, Jake tended to sleep in his clothes on top of the covers, a little concerned at what he might find when he pulled them down. However, over time he came to find that the hotel was worn but reasonably clean, putting Jake's mind more at ease. Even so, out in the city was always much more exciting and stimulating than the bleak room.

Even in his short time in the city he had already experienced some of the good and the bad that the place had to offer. He listened to a concert in the park and marveled at all the different nationalities and types of people he saw, some relaxing while some danced along to the band. Others played chess and dominoes at permanently installed tables suited just for those games. He even saw people in deep meditation right in the middle of the music and hustle and bustle. Jake wondered how they were not distracted by it all. Wonderful smells from food shops and carts also filled the air. It seemed to Jake that anything anyone could ever desire was right there.

He also witnessed homelessness for the first time, and aggressive panhandlers harassing visitors to the City as easy prey. Other people he encountered, in stark contrast to those at the park, seemed to just be angry. Plenty of people always seemed to be in a giant hurry, and were not afraid to let anyone slowing them down know about it. At times, all of this made him miss his peaceful grove of trees, as well as his friend Red.

Finding work in Pine Grove at the camp and the store had come fairly easy to him. His search for employment in the city was more difficult than he had expected. Some places were not looking for someone that didn't have a certain look, and others wouldn't even talk to him without a college degree. He found a job in sales, but was quickly dismissed for not being aggressive enough. Another potential opportunity was snatched away overnight when the owner of the company was arrested out of the blue.

Jake persevered, however, and finally did manage to find employment at a small hole-in-the-wall, greasy spoon restaurant with cuisine that included a few Greek, Turkish, and Italian staples. The Athena was named by the previous owner. It had a storefront straight out of the 50's, and showed every phase of renovation in some manner in the small interior. Dark wood tables and chairs that looked like they were original to the place, amber glass wall sconces, round globe lamps hanging from the ceiling over each table and the counter, and some past variation of speckled tile flooring that likely contained asbestos. The only modern feature in the interior was the bright, neon 'open' sign hung in the window expected to entice potential diners to look past the facade.

The Athena was part of an eclectic neighborhood that was in transition as evident by a neighboring modern coffee shop, classic delicatessen, and ancient shoemaker shop.

Jake responded to the 'help wanted' sign in the window. The cook looked Jake up and down to size him up. After pausing he asked, "you been arrested? I don't want that hassle."

"No." replied Jake.

"You ever work in a restaurant?" was his next question.

Jake replied with "sorta," adding, "I worked in a cafeteria and performed maintenance at a scout camp. I understand how to work with food, follow directions, and can do basic wiring, plumbing, and repair if that helps."

The cook raised his eyebrows slightly after Jake's last comment. "Ok, I'll give you a shot. We are a small place, just myself, a waitress, and a busboy most days. Not enough business to need much more, but I always want someone else to know things in case something happens. We all do everything sometimes, and are only open for lunch and dinner. We also are open 6 days a week, closed Mondays...can you do that?"

"Absolutely!" replied Jake who was happy to get anything to provide some income. He also wanted to stay busy to keep his mind from home and Red.

"Good. My name is Deniz. My cousin and I own this place. You can start tomorrow."

*　　　　*　　　　*

Jake arrived early for his first day at The Athena. The first few days were just he, Deniz, and another employee named Pedro. Pedro seemed to do a little bit of everything in the restaurant including busboy, stocker, and food prep. Jake liked the idea of being able to pitch in where needed. He handled his expected jobs easily, such as carrying and putting deliveries away and cleaning the restaurant after hours. He delivered food to the tables, as well as refilled drinks. At one point he even filled in on food prep because there were actually three parties eating at the same time. "We got a rush!" Pedro joked to Deniz who only raised a single eyebrow in response. Deniz handled the waiter duties, leaving Jake to wonder if the waitress he had been told about had already quit.

For most days that first week he and Pedro cleaned after closing. One evening Deniz stayed late so that the three of them could deep clean the kitchen. Jake used their time together to learn a little about the neighborhood.

"Is a good neighborhood," Deniz offered first, "lots of variety. Not too far from subway lines into the city. Good people, for the most part."

Pedro added, "yeah, it's ok, but not as nice as my beloved Queens."

"Your beloved Queens," Deniz repeated with a smile on his face, "you commute here every day from that place. Why do you not move closer and save yourself that hassle?"

"Hassle? No hassle, 'cause Queens is where it's *at*," Pero replied emphatically.

Jake interjected, "I'm not ready for Queens, I still have to learn about here."

"You want to learn about here, talk to old man Johnson over at the smoke shop. He's been here forever, knows everyone," Pedro replied, "of course it will cost you. Everything is overpriced at his place, know what I'm sayin'?"

"It is not that bad," Deniz replied, again jokingly contradicting Pedro.

"Well, if you paid me more, maybe I could afford his place," Pedro joked back.

"Any other people that have been here forever?" Jake asked.

"A few that I know of, but most of them are pretty old so you don't really see them out much," Deniz replied.

"The mobsters are still around," Pedro added. Deniz immediately shot a look at Pedro.

"Mobsters?" Jake asked, "Really? Like in the Sopranos?"

"Yes, they are around," Deniz relented, "but they aren't really an issue. The Mob used to be all over this neighborhood in the past, but not so much now."

"You're fooling him again," Pedro remarked, "that family was big time, and their bosses are out of jail running them again."

"What were they in jail for, or don't I want to know?" Jake asked.

"RICO rounded up a bunch of Mob bosses back in the 80s. Guys served their time and are getting out now," Pedro replied.

"Didn't that bring down the Mafia?" Jake asked, trying to recall from the Modern American History course he took as a Senior.

"Take them down? No way. Might have messed them up some and made them change tactics, but the bigger families were plenty deep and stepped in to take over until the bosses got released."

"Alright, enough Mafia talk," Deniz interrupted, "don't worry about them, stay away from the delicatessen and you should be fine."

"The delicatessen? You mean like across the street?!" Jake asked with concern.

"Yeah, that's one of the places that they hang out. Just stay away and you should be fine," Deniz instructed.

After a long pause Jake asked, "so, do they ever come in here to eat?"

"Jake, hardly anyone comes in here to eat, you think that they would choose this over somewhere else?" Pedro responded, again receiving a glare from Deniz who walked out of the kitchen to tend to something in the front of the restaurant.

"Well, I guess it's good that they aren't as big as they once were," Jake commented to Pedro, more to convince himself.

"Yeah, they aren't what they were, but don't underestimate them. You hear stories about them from back in the day. Working protection and muscle for the big families, they could be ice cold, man. But don't think that is all gone. I heard that one of them killed a guy he suspected of talking to the cops a few years back. Got him at his mistress's. Shot her, shot him, and then even shot her little dog and shoved it in the guy's mouth. Old school guys would shove a rat in someone's mouth when they killed them for talking. This guy shoved the little dog in there. Probably found it funny. Freakin' crazy, is what it is. I heard it was the grandson of the boss, too. And he's still out there."

Jake paused on this for another beat. "Ok, stay away from the deli. Got it. I'm never going there," he replied.

Deniz reentered the kitchen, saying "I better not be hearing any more talk about the mobsters." Pedro and Jake got the message and returned their attention to cleaning.

On day six the mystery waitress showed up. She was average height, petite in frame, and a few years older than Jake. Her dark, curly hair was up in a hair tie, and she had a tattoo on the inside of her right forearm. She had striking features, but her eyes were swollen and tired, and her shoulders pitched forward slightly as if holding up an enormous weight. Her uniform consisted of black leggings, a black t-shirt, and scuffed white sneakers. She already had a pen in her hair at the ready.

Deniz made their introduction. "Sarah, this is the new guy, Jake." Sarah glanced up and smiled through her weariness.

"Nice to meet you, I'm Jake," Jake offered.

"Hi. Sarah," was Sarah's simple reply, as she quickly went back to wrapping silverware in a paper napkin, leaving Jake staring at her absentmindedly.

Deniz broke the pause, "We are trying him out to see if he can fill in around here." Sarah responded with a subtle nod while she focused on her task.

"Well, ok then..." Jake replied to no one in particular, going back to wiping down the chairs and tables.

As Jake turned, Sarah looked up and followed Jake with an inquisitive look as he walked away and started working again. After contemplating a few seconds, a small smile grew on her face as she turned her focus back on her tasks.

9

"Nina and I can handle it, Father. We're fine." Meya proclaimed. "You just don't get this world...I do!"

Meya Chang had just finished her four-year degree at Berkshire College, majoring in Art. In her mind, that made her an expert. She had been on track to be a Russian literature expert and then a botany expert, but each of those majors had only lasted one year.

Meya's father, Jiao Chang, fully financed his daughter's journey. A wealthy businessman, Jiao had met Meya's mother, Catherine, when she worked in his country teaching English. Jiao and Catherine loved their only daughter, and always provided their full financial support despite nearly constant reservations about their daughter's next endeavor.

The main reason Meya had stayed an art major the full four years was her attachment to her professor, Dr. Chad Longfellow. Dr. Longfellow was in his late thirties, loved to dress in the proper professor manner, including tweed sports coats with patch elbows and cashmere scarves no matter what the weather, and encouraged his favorite students to fondly refer to him simply as 'Chad'. Ivy league educated, Chad was a fairly talented artist. He was mainly a painter, and had some connections in the art world made through academic and professional associations. Chad loved to be on the pedestal and always seemed to gravitate to the most admiring, and arguably most naive, students.

Meya hung on Chad's every word, eventually forming a view on art that not surprisingly aligned very closely with Chad's. Their relationship was strictly professional except when it was otherwise, usually stemming from convenience or fueled by alcohol and weed. On more than one occasion Meya woke in the bed of her professor, both of them swearing that it would never happen again, until it did.

Now Meya was in the city. She had decided, after a few discussions with Chad, to open her own gallery. Her roommate, Nina Blum, had majored in business. The two had decided that their combined knowledge, along with help from Chad, was enough to successfully open and operate the gallery. Meya's father's financing would, in reality, be the biggest contributing factor.

Meya, Nina, Jiao, and Catherine were exploring a potential space for the gallery. The loft was on the third floor. With high ceilings that exposed the steel beams of the floor above and large windows on the two corner walls, the space lent itself to the open gallery. The long plank flooring was remnant of the building's past life, fortunately saved and restored. The white walls were already framed to accommodate a hanging system for the pieces, and the ceiling and beams had been painted black to keep the viewer's eyes on the art. Ample outlets and track lighting were the final element of the interior.

The C-shaped layout of the main viewing area wrapped around a small office, bathroom, and storage room. Two legs of the viewing area were on outer walls in the building's corner. The other leg had a large, sliding, red metal door as the entrance leading to a small lobby connecting the gallery to the other spaces. The lobby contained the main elevator and access to the stairwell. A less attractive sliding door in the back of the small storage area opened into a short hallway, the freight elevator, and outside to the fire escape metal balcony.

"You do not have the experience necessary to form a successful gallery," Jiao said, expressing some of his concerns to his daughter. "You know nothing about business or the things that are needed."

"Nina knows it all, Father. Tell her Nina," Meya commanded.

"Um, well, sir, not only did I major in business, but I helped to manage my father's hardware store back in Pennsylvania," Nina said.

"Selling screwdrivers is not the same as selling art," Jiao responded.

"I know sir, but there are similarities. We will sell on consignment, just like at the store. We will market online as well, an area that was very important to our store because it specialized in advanced commercial flooring systems. We also will utilize similar bookkeeping and accounting methods."

"Sell on consignment? Who will consign art to you two? You are both too young and inexperienced."

"Chad….er, my professor has connections, Father. Plus, we will sell my art and his as well," Meya interjected.

"The cost of this space is very high. Will this professor's art sell for a high enough price? What does he do?" Jiao asked.

"He paints, Father, his work is displayed at the College and in several exhibits." Meya added, neglecting to include the fact that the exhibits were local and sponsored by the school, as well as a few small shows local to the College.

"So, this entire thing, all of the cost, all of the risk is riding on the paintings of your professor and your art?" Jiao asked, having never understood his daughter's modern, eccentric pieces. "This does not sound good to me, not at all," Jiao said. All of his business instincts told him this was a bad idea.

"Father," Meya said softly as she smoothed her voice and wrapped her hand around her father's arm. "I know I have changed my mind in the past, but I really want this. Art is my life now, and I know that I can do this. Please Father, please reconsider for me?"

At this point Jiao usually folded to his daughter's desires. He was never able to say no to her, his only daughter. He looked at his wife who looked back knowingly. She had seen this play out before and knew where it was headed. Surprisingly, however, Jiao's reply this time was not an outright 'yes'.

"I will talk to the landlord. I will give you one month to make this gallery work. One month to find art, one month to establish the business. Product, marketing, delivery, security, all of it. One month is all."

"But Father, that is not enough time! We need more than a month to get all of that together. It's not fair," a shocked and sullen Meya replied.

Jiao was expecting this knowing that they would actually have three months, as that was the shortest lease that he had already negotiated with the landlord.

"Fine, you have two months, my daughter. Now, we go."

10

Jake didn't mind the work at the restaurant, but he didn't care much for the boredom. Jake would clean the entire restaurant each day even if there had only been a few patrons. He had repaired a few wobbly tables, the thermometer embedded in the refrigerator door, and a leaking faucet in the men's bathroom. He took pride in his work, and probably more importantly to his limited savings, wanted to make sure he was able to keep the job. This and his other tasks took up some of his day, but at times left too much free time allowing his mind to wander.

Jake wondered how his mother and Red were doing, especially during these down times. He still felt leaving had been the right thing to do, but he didn't especially like how he did it. The full head of steam that drove him out of the hospital was still there when he went to tell his mother he was leaving. She was in tears when he rode away, knowing he wasn't angry at her, but angry, nonetheless. As he pulled from their driveway he did stop, pull back in, and hug his mother telling her he loved her and would be ok. He could still see the sadness and trepidation in her weak smile as he rode off.

Jake decided to call his mother using the restaurant's phone. After a few rings she picked up, ecstatic to hear her son's voice. Jake.

"Hi Mom," Jake said, immediately having to pull the receiver away to shield his ear from his mother's enthusiastic salutation. "It's good to hear your voice too...yes, I'm fine...yes, Mom, I'm eating, in fact I work in a restaurant...I'm not sure how long...Mom, how's Red?" Jake didn't realize that he was gripping the receiver so tightly that his knuckles had turned white. "...alive, he's alive? Have you seen him?...ok, sure, but let me know when you do...Mom, I love you...Mom, please don't cry, I'll call you again soon, promise...Bye Mom, take care and thanks for the good news." Jake sat in the office, stunned, holding the receiver in his hand until a screeching tone shrieked from the earpiece. *'Red's alive'*, he thought. As the reality set in he felt a lightness and energy that he hadn't felt in a long time. *'Red's alive!'*

Jake returned the receiver to the phone's cradle and jumped from the chair all in one motion. He glided through the kitchen and into the dining room. Over the course of the first few weeks the free time gave him a chance to get to know Pedro and Sarah. Pedro tended to work in the kitchen with Deniz, and hung out there mostly. Sarah and Jake spent most of their time in the front waiting on, or for, customers. Up to this point most of their discussions had focused on the restaurant, the city, and other superficial topics. Buoyed by his mother's good news about Red, Jake finally decided to try to learn more about Sarah.

He approached her in the dining room, with a playful spring in his step and a mischievous smile, saying, "So, I think that it's fine time that we learn a bit about Sarah."

Sarah looked at him with a puzzled look, "Are you ok? You're acting strange."

Jake replied quickly, "Right as rain, ma'am. Now, let's get started. Are you from around here?"

"No, West Virginia," Sarah replied, still skeptical but curious, and determined not to allow the impending line of questioning to be one-sided, "You?"

"Vermont. I guess that we're both aliens in a strange land." Jake said, feeling like his enthusiasm was starting to make him sound crazy. "So, you're from the country, like me?" he quickly asked to try to recover.

"Yeah. A small place. My family has been there for generations," Sarah replied, blowing a stray strand of hair out of her face, with a crooked smile forming in reaction to Jake's behavior.

'*This is going ok*', Jake thought, readying himself for his next question.

Before the conversation could continue, the door flew open and a hulking man burst in. "Where is he, where is my cousin?!" he asked loudly. The man had a Turkish accent, and his booming voice filled the entire space.

Deniz called from the kitchen. "Hello Cousin," he said, trying little to hide his annoyance knowing that an argument was likely coming.

Zehab Barak was a large man, with thick black hair cut short that was graying around his ears, heavy dark eyebrows, and the largest, densest black mustache that Jake had ever seen. He wore a light purple collared shirt unbuttoned to the fourth button exposing a thick mat of graying chest hair, a thin jacket, and gray slacks. His loafers appeared to Jake to be made from the leather of a scaled animal, such as alligator, and were dyed a shade that complimented his shirt. His presence in the room held everyone's attention, even the two patrons eating at a corner table.

Zehab stormed into the kitchen and started to yell at his cousin. It was loud enough that everyone in the small dining area could hear. "You're at it again. Why can you not just make the food like our grandmother made it, and stop trying to pretend you are a real chef? None of this food tastes right. Cousin, you are a bum just like me. The only difference is that I got the brains to make business work. For shit's sake, she gave you her cookbook. Make it like she wrote it, and stop thinking that you have the brains to do more than that."

Deniz and his cousin had countless arguments over the years on a variety of subjects. He replied, raising his voice, but not shouting. "You have been talking to me that way since we were small boys. Always you boast of how smart you are, what a great businessman you are. Well, you would not have *any* of it if it weren't for me doing the work. Me marching like a good little soldier. And for what? For you to yell at me anytime I try something new to improve and bring in more customers?"

Zehab reacted instantly, "No! We are not having this discussion again. I am done carrying you. Your behaviors not only cost me money each time, but are now risking my other ventures too. Not this time Cousin…do it right or you and I are done."

This argument was clearly different, but Deniz, stunned a bit but still pridefully maintaining a rigid posture, was not going to have any of it. "Oh really Cousin? And I am the risk? You squander every business you take on. None of them work, and you never do anything to fix it. *You* are done?...*I* am done! Good luck making any of this work without me." Letting his speech hang for just a second, Deniz took off his apron and threw it on the counter next to Zehab, never once breaking eye contact with his cousin. He then turned on his heel and walked out of the kitchen.

The two customers had quickly exited when the shouting started. Jake and Sarah just stared as Deniz stormed out of the kitchen never once looking back as he exited the restaurant.

Zehab entered the dining area with an unsure look on his face, "What a fool. He will be back. Thinks that he knows more than me, that he can be the brains behind the operation.

He should think again! Fool." As he rubbed his chin Zehab continued, "Besides, I really don't need him."

Finally noticing Jake and Sarah, Zehab's orders were simple, "Don't you have work to do?" He pointed to Sarah, "Clean this room and prep for tomorrow. And you," he said turning to Jake, "go and clean the kitchen."

At this, Zehab stormed through the restaurant and out the front door. Sarah and Jake immediately took to their assignments.

11

Jake surveyed the kitchen. It smelled slightly of burnt grease, but nothing rotten or out of the ordinary. The stainless steel appliances lined one wall. A warmer oven located in the corner next to a wash sink, followed by a prep counter with cabinets below and a shelf of labeled containers with spices above. Beside the prep area were the main cooking appliances, a deep fryer, a griddle, and a six burner Viking gas range and oven which was dated but in good working order. Above the range was a stainless vent equipped with the standard fire suppression system required by the city. Spoons and ladles hung from the end of the vent, and a long knife holder was mounted on the subway tile wall near the prep area. On another wall separated from the cooking area was the industrial side-by-side refrigerator and freezer. A narrow staging table sat in the middle of the kitchen.

Jake spent about an hour cleaning the kitchen, even though it was already pretty clean. When he was done, Jake turned his attention from the kitchen to the dry storage area in the back of the restaurant, which only really needed to be swept.

Jake leaned into the makeshift office in the back of the storage area to see if there was any general cleaning that he could perform. The place was a mess. A small desk with built-in shelves above was covered in papers. The old wooden desk chair had wheels and swiveled, but looked like it hadn't moved in a decade. Even if someone had wanted to move the chair, space was limited. Several boxes, including a few without lids, were piled along one wall. Jake swept his broom over the exposed floor of the office collecting as much dust as he had in the rest of the kitchen and storage area combined.

Jake didn't dare touch the desk for fear of messing up some sort of secret filing system, but decided that there would probably be no harm re-stacking the pile of boxes. He had removed the first two when he heard a thud as something fell to the floor behind the pile. After removing a few more boxes Jake was able to reach his arm far down between the remaining pile and the wall, reaching almost to the floor. As he scratched at first at air, he finally made contact with an object. After he repositioned his arm he was able to get a good grip, retrieving an old book.

The book was very dusty with a browning cover that appeared to be wooden with a few remnants of printed letters and decoration that was too faded to decipher. It was more a set of papers bound with loose loops of string than a typically bound volume. After wiping the dust from the cover, Jake opened the book. The page had an entry of neatly written characters, more symbols than letters, with a single signature at the bottom of the page. As Jake started to look at other pages he came to realize this was a recipe book with each recipe entered neatly with the symbolic writing, and with what Jake assumed was the English translation scratched coarsely next to each line.

Jake realized almost instantly that this was probably the recipe book that Zehab had pointed out to his cousin. He ran quickly to the dining room with the book, excited to show Sarah. "I think that this is it!" he said excitedly.

"Is what?" Sarah inquired, turning from wiping a table.

"The recipe book...the one that Zehab was talking about."

Sarah looked down at the book in his hands. Jake moved next to Sarah and began to flip through the pages. They flipped through recipes for Şakşuka, Iskemper Kebap, and Turkish Manti, finally stopping on Moussaka. "This is actually on the menu," Sarah noted.

"Want to try to make it?" Jake asked.

Jake and Sarah looked at each other. It was getting late, and they were not sure what tomorrow would bring at The Athena. Figuring that they really had nothing to lose Sarah replied resolutely, "Sure, why not."

They found all of the ingredients in the kitchen. Jake fried the eggplant and started browning the beef while Sarah chopped the vegetables and found the spices. Together they layered the pan and poured in the blended beef, vegetables, and spices and put it in the oven.

While they cleaned up Jake decided that it might be a safe time to find out some more about Sarah. "So, West Virginia," he offered, waiting to see how Sarah reacted.

"Yup, take me home country roads and everything," she replied, evidently enjoying her time cooking with Jake.

"What brought you to the city?" Jake asked, deciding that it might be safe to venture a little farther.

"It was time to leave," Sarah replied simply.

Jake smiled to himself. He had told himself those same words when it was time for him to leave Pine Grove. He continued to stare at the bowl that he was drying, waiting to see if Sarah would continue, which she did.

"Have you ever gotten yourself into a situation and have no real idea how it happened?" Sarah asked. "Well, if I'm being honest with myself, I know how it happened. Pick the best looking guy with the best looking car around, the bad boy, and I shouldn't be surprised where things ended up. But I am surprised, actually." Sarah finished hanging the dried mixing spoons and turned to Jake. "I don't know why I'm telling you this. I'm sorry, you probably don't want to hear all this, I'm sure."

Jake hung the towel over his shoulder and jumped up to seat himself on the staging table. "I have a while until the food is done, so of course I don't mind," he said in the most charming way that he could muster.

Sarah smiled at his humor, and continued with almost a tone of relief in her voice, like she had kept this story hidden away and was finally able to release it. "We dated for two years before things started to change. In that time we never had any problems. He would run around with his car buddies sometimes all night, but I never heard of him fooling around on me or getting arrested or anything." Sarah leaned against the stove prep area across from Jake.

"Then he lost his job. After a few months we were running out of money to pay rent, keep the electricity on, that kind of stuff. I told him I would ask my family for a loan, but there was no way he was going to allow that, especially since they already didn't care for him. His evenings out with the boys started to end up more at the bar and less working in someone's garage."

At this Sarah looked down and paused for several beats. Jake waited patiently allowing her to collect her thoughts.

When she looked up she had tears welling in her eyes. "Things were starting to really get desperate. One morning he came home after a night of carrying on. I told him that something had to give, and that maybe he should sell his Camaro to get us some money. I'll never forget the rage in his eyes when he looked up at me." Sarah was starting to shake slightly and had her arms crossed tightly. Even so, Jake felt that it was best not to move or interrupt, taking a page from what Red had taught him about grieving and needing to sometimes just let the emotion and words finally come out.

Sarah took a long deep breath trying to keep her composure. "Then, he just hit me. I was knocked to the floor. He just stood over me and said, 'It will never be you over my car.' Then he bent and threatened, 'and don't even think of leaving and running back home to mommy and daddy. I'll get to you, that's a promise.'"

Sarah now had tears streaming down her cheek.

She turned at this point and stared directly at Jake, asserting in a voice filled with hurt and pain. "He chose that stupid car over me!" Jake knew the sharing was over at this point. He jumped down from the counter and put his arms around Sarah who held her arms folded tightly and sobbed into Jake's chest.

12

Jake held Sarah for several minutes. As Jake loosened his hold of Sarah he looked into her eyes, saying, "No one deserves to be treated like that, especially you." Sarah smiled slightly as the two gazed deeply at each other.

At that moment the timer on Jake's watch chimed, breaking their gaze.

"I guess it's done," Sarah said, unfolding her folded arms and wiping the tears quickly from her eyes.

"Um, I guess so," replied Jake.

"I'll go clean myself up and get some plates. We can eat in the dining room properly," Sarah said as she started to walk away, still touching her eyes with her fingertips.

Jake felt both exhilarated and dazed at the same time. Collecting himself, he took the pan of cooked moussaka out of the oven and carried it to the dining room. Sarah had set out two plates, unwrapped two sets of silverware, and had partially filled two glasses with red wine. She was already sitting at one of the places, across from the other setting for Jake.

Jake served each of them, and then sat down to join her. Jake raised his glass for a toast, "Here's to new beginnings," which Sarah finished with "And the new friends that come with them," before tapping her glass on Jake's.

Sarah tried her meal first. "Mmmm, this is delicious," was her first comment with a look of satisfaction and surprise on her face. After savoring the bite she added, "this is much better than what Deniz serves. Zehab is right." Jake took a bite as well. The deep rich flavor immediately struck him, as the food and Sarah's company warmed him all over.

Jake and Sarah finished their portions, but continued to talk as light rain began to fall outside. Neither of them noticed the raindrops running down the glass until they heard the knock on the door, looking over to see Zehab peering through the window. Sarah looked at Jake, and then rose walking to the door to unlock it and let Zehab in. "What are you two still doing here?" he asked, evidently intoxicated but calmer than earlier. He continued without waiting for an answer, "We will not be opening tomorrow. We have no cook. I am not sure we will be able to stay open."

Zehab finished his thought as he slumped into a chair a few tables from theirs lowering his head into the palms of his hands. "I will have to find another way to support my businesses sooner than I thought."

Zehab's dulled senses from the several Raki and Efes Pilsens consumed over the course of the evening suddenly kicked in. "What is that smell?" he asked, lifting his head from his hands.

"Moussaka," Sarah replied.

"It smells wonderful," Zehab said, inhaling deeply.

"Want some?" asked Jake, as Sarah rushed off to grab a plate and set of silverware. Not waiting for an answer, Jake cut a square from the pan using his knife and placed it on the plate using his unused spoon. Sarah placed the served dish and unwrapped silverware in front of Zehab, who had sat up to admire it.

Zehab tilted his head to look at the side of the moussaka, then touched the top lightly with his fork as if checking to see if it had the proper stiffness. Next, he bent closer, almost touching his mustache to the food, and waved his free hand towards his nose to ensure he captured the aroma. Zehab finally cut a corner from the square and lifted it to his mouth. At first he did not chew, but let the food sit on his tongue as he closed his eyes for a second. He then started to chew and nod, his eyes opening and a smile forming on his face as he swallowed.

"This is it," he said evenly and calmly, looking at Sarah. "This is how my grandmother made it."

"He made it," Sarah said, pointing at Jake.

Sarah and Zehab turned to look at Jake. "When did you go to Turkey? You must have visited my country to make this so perfectly. Turkey is a beautiful country, do you not agree?" Zehab asked, the effects of the alcohol and Turkish food making him nostalgic for home.

"Turkey?? I've never even left Pine Grove," Jake responded.

"Ahh, where is this Pine Grove, and is it beautiful there as well?" Zehab asked in a boisterous voice with a broad wave of his hand towards Jake, continuing his intoxicated ramblings.

"Vermont," Jake replied, "and yes, it is beautiful."

"Well, Jake from Vermont, this is delicious. Tell me, how did you learn to make it?"

"I just followed the recipe in the book," Jake responded, his eyes wide, a little bit nervous and unsure of what exactly was going to happen next.

Zehab rose with a smile, grabbing Jake's shoulders in his huge hands. "The book...the book? What is this book? Here? Can you bring it to me?"

"An old cookbook that I found behind a box in the office. I wasn't snooping, honestly, I was just trying to clean like you told me to."

"No worry, my boy. Go, and bring it to me," Zehab said as gently as he could muster, removing his hands from Jake's shoulders.

Jake went to the kitchen, returning with the cookbook. Zehab cradled the book in his hands, looking at it as one would a newborn. "This is it. You have found it. That idiot Deniz either lost it or tried to hide it from me, but you found it. Not only did you find it, but you cooked the Moussaka the way it is supposed to be made." A giant smile grew on Zehab's face.

Zehab startled both Jake and Sarah, making them jump slightly as he smacked Jake on the shoulder. "You. You will be the cook. We will *not* close. Take that Deniz! We open tomorrow as any other day with you as cook. Excellent."

Zehab put the book down on the table and pulled his collar up. "Good," he said again quietly, as if convincing himself. As he started to walk towards the door, he paused and turned back to them. "And what is your name?" he asked.

"Sarah," Sarah replied in a fairly monotone fashion.

"Jake and Sarah. Good. I will see you tomorrow," Zehab replied as he walked out into the night.

Jake and Sarah turned and looked at each other in disbelief, each trying to grasp what had just happened.

They quickly returned to the kitchen and worked the entire night to prepare as many dishes in the cookbook as they could find ingredients, focusing on dishes that could be heated the next day. They failed at several the first time, but didn't seem to mind. They both seemed to be content just working in each other's company.

This time the conversation stayed light. Jake told her a bit about Vermont and the camp. He didn't mention Red or even his father's death. He focused on the landscape and his experiences in the outdoors. "Vermont sounds a lot like West Virginia," Sarah commented, "except that you don't get the joy of black coal dust that doesn't wash out of anything."

Sarah kept her sharing light as well. Talk of family and friends at times, but more about how different the city is from where she grew up. She didn't revisit her past this time. Jake didn't care what she talked about, he just enjoyed getting to know anything about her.

They were just finishing cleaning as the sun came up. They both decided that a few hours of sleep would probably do them good before their first day of attempting to keep the restaurant open. Heading their separate ways Jake called out to Sarah, "That was fun, thanks. See you in a few hours." Sarah replied wittingly, "Not if I see you first."

13

Things were going well at the restaurant. Zehab had not returned since the night that he had tried Jake's cooking and promoted him to head cook. Sarah had smartly reduced the menu to only a handful of items, many that could be prepared in larger amounts and used for several servings. Jake and Sarah were also happy to learn that Pedro hadn't been just hanging out in the kitchen, but had at times also been handling some of the ordering and bill payment for Deniz. Pedro ended up being a pretty handy assistant to Jake in the kitchen at times, as well.

While business had not increased noticeably, it also hadn't really decreased either which meant that The Athena stayed open and the three of them remained employed.

The Athena was closed on Mondays. Sarah and Jake had gotten closer, but their budding friendship, or more as Jake secretly hoped, was limited to their time together in the restaurant. The previous Saturday after the restaurant had closed and the three worked to finish cleaning and prep for the next day, Pedro asked about Jake's favorite part of being in the city. Jake chuckled, replying, "I don't know. Other than the little exploring that I did when I first arrived, the only places that I spend most of my time are the restaurant, my room at the Elm Tree Inn, and the laundromat down the street."

Sarah's reply came immediately, "Are you serious? You came to the city, but you haven't done anything? Ok, then,

Monday you and I are going to do some more exploring. I'll be your tour guide and we'll check out the neighborhood...sound good?"

Jake's heart leapt in his chest with excitement. Two thoughts immediately popped into his mind. The first, dizzying excitement at the prospect of spending the day with Sarah. The second was the realization that Pedro might want to tag along and he wouldn't be spending the day with just Sarah. As he thought the latter, he turned to make eye contact with Pedro who already knew what Jake was thinking.

"Aww, man, I'm out for Monday. Cousin and I have a thing. Catch you next time?" Pedro said, while smiling at Jake.

"Ok then," Sarah replied, "I guess it's just you and me then, you in?"

"Sounds good," Jake replied, as he watched Pedro offer him the slightest head nod and eyebrow raise to go with his smile. He then looked at Sarah who was looking back and smiling as well.

*   *   *

Sarah and Jake toured the neighborhood, winding their way through the streets with no real destination in mind. Sarah had been busy earlier in the day, so they didn't set out until the afternoon. Jake marveled at the variety of people that he saw, typical of a neighborhood in the process of renewal. He appreciated how there were people of all different ages, races, and nationalities coexisting in such a small area. He knew it was different from the days that he had learned about in school when neighborhoods were primarily made up of similar nationalities and everyone knew everyone else, essential to survival at the time.

He was also fascinated by the architecture and functionality of the place. Storefronts ranging from old doorways with half-pane windows and hand painted signs to the latest flashy full storefronts with bright branding and large posters of tantalizing food and coffee. He paused, his attention on the old lady sweeping her walk with a straw broom, now several inches shorter from use, who probably understood the history of the neighborhood better than most. The ever-evolving aromas as they walked, ranging from the sweet smells of the pastry shop to the strong distinct smell of incense and candles from the yoga studio. All of this was accented by a near constant hum of the traffic making its way to each important destination.

At one building Sarah noticed a sign advertising a reception for the grand opening of a new art gallery, View. The sign offered the enticing reward of free hors d'oeuvres and drinks for anyone that chose to join them for their celebration.

"Oh, nice. Free food and drink. What do you think, interested in stopping in?" Sarah asked.

Not being the least bit interested in art, but very interested in Sarah, Jake responded, "Sure, let's go see some art!" in a mildly mocking tone as he opened and held the door for Sarah.

"Don't dismiss too quickly Vermont boy, you might just find something that you like," Sarah quipped.

"Yeah, free food," Jake replied entering the building after her.

They entered the gallery space, and were greeted by a small, round table with a few brochures and business cards.

There were a handful of people in attendance. Before they had an opportunity to look around, a woman came to greet them. "Hello and welcome. I'm Nina. Meya, the owner, had to step out, but I wanted to be sure and welcome you to View."

"Thanks," replied Sarah.

"Please take your time and have a look around. There are some drinks and bites near the window in the front. Help yourself, and please feel free to ask any questions," Nina offered.

"Ok, well, thanks again," Sarah again replied simply, trying to head off a potential hard sell from Nina, "we'll take a look around."

Nina left them quickly, obviously not very comfortable in the role of host. Sarah and Jake slowly made their way around the space. Sarah paused at a few of the pieces, exploring them with her eyes. Jake looked at a few but always seemed to find himself checking out the mechanics of how the spaced worked. He found himself inspecting the hanging system for the wall pieces, the glass enclosed gallery pillars positioned under a few of the pieces, and the mechanism providing an assist when opening the large, red metal door through which they entered.

Eventually they made their way to the food and drink which consisted of some warm filled pastry, vegetables, and cookies from a local bakery. The food was complemented by sparkling grape juice already poured and warming in glasses, as well as several bottles of water. "Well, this is a letdown," Sarah commented quietly to Jake, "sometimes these spreads are great. All of this money hanging on the wall and in those cases, and they serve this cut rate stuff. How do they ever expect to make it in the gallery world?" she continued as if she knew the secret to establishing a successful gallery.

After they each had a few bites of food and some sparkling grape juice from plastic champagne flutes they headed out. As they left Nina called to them, "Thanks for coming, and remember to tell your friends."

Jake just thought to himself, *'Don't hold your breath Nina, I won't be back.'*

They ate at a small place a few blocks from The Athena, and then found themselves walking through a park that connected various parts of the city. Paved walks meandered from neighborhood to neighborhood lined with plantings and featuring busts of leaders local to each connected part of the city. They were really beginning to enjoy each other's company, and Sarah was especially happy that they were able to do so outside of work for a change. She was still on guard for people changing when the situation changed, but Jake seemed to be a stand-up guy who worked hard, seemed gentle, and genuinely enjoyed her.

As they walked and the sun began to set, Sarah finally mustered the courage to ask, "Ok Jake, so what brought you to the city."

Jake knew that this question would come at some point as he and Sarah grew closer. "It was time for me to leave, as well," he replied. As they strolled Jake told Sarah about Pine Grove. He talked about the loss of his father, the toll it took on him and his mother, and then how he had found Red.

Red...Jake hadn't thought of him in several days. *'How could I not think about Red?'*, he wondered to himself. He had immersed himself in his success at the restaurant and budding relationship with Sarah. Jake knew in his heart this is what Red wanted for him all along. Red wanted Jake to be able to break free of the pain of his past. To be able to move on, never forgetting but not dwelling. Even so, Jake still felt for his friend as he wondered how he was doing, if his mother had been able to visit him, and if he would even be able to recover to the man he was before the accident.

As Jake finished telling Sarah about how Red had been there for him, mentoring him, and then how the explosion had almost taken Red's life, he realized that Sarah was holding his hand. Jake hadn't even noticed, but was happy that it was happening. As Jake finished talking, they walked along in silence as the sun disappeared and night started to take its turn. As they reached a small lookout area, Jake turned to face Sarah. She looked up at him with softer features than before, as if she had found a kindred soul, someone that maybe she could start to believe in again. Jake bent to kiss Sarah, who returned the affection. After they kissed Jake said softly, "I'm glad that I found you."

Sarah whispered, "I'm glad I found you too."

14

Johnny 'The Jeweler' Stints stood in the corner of the new art gallery, View. Sonny had issued a standing order that he should always scope out any new commercial business for potential opportunities for the family. In actuality Louie had pointed this place out to Johnny. Even though Louie wasn't of pure Italian descent, and would never be a made guy as a result, he had a keen feel for the neighborhood. He had turned Sonny's crew on to several opportunities over the few years he had worked with them. He also had good street crime and survival skills, assets always sought out in the world of organized crime.

Open houses always made the scoping effort easier and less conspicuous. View was the latest thing to open in the neighborhood, a sparse space with art hanging on the wall and in cases. Johnny had eaten a few of the pastries and choked down a glass of some bubbly apple tasting stuff that clearly wasn't champagne. There were only a few other people at the grand opening. *'Not a good sign'*, Johnny thought.

Johnny put his skills to use, scouting the place for entry and exit opportunities and easy ways to separate the owner from their wares in a manner that they wouldn't notice. He even managed to pace the timing of when the single employee, a woman named Nina, was talking to another person to slip into the back room for a quick look.

He scanned the storage room as well as the office and back entry door. There was no safe evident in the back, meaning that none of the pieces were put under extra lock and key at night. There also did not appear to be any cash on the premises, not that he expected it in an art gallery, but he always made sure to check. His biggest note was that there were no security cameras or any sign of a security system. '*Pretty perfect*', thought Johnny. '*An easy in and out job to grab a few pieces, no doubt.*' The only concern would be if someone noticed their shadows moving around in the spaces at night, illuminated from the street and city lights. '*Low risk*', Johnny thought since the gallery was up a few floors. Timing would be everything. Robberies also did a nice job of motivating people to pay for protection, which the Amoretti family would be happy to provide for a price. '*A win-win.*'

Johnny didn't know if the business was financially sound, but suspected that it was not this early in its existence. He wanted to keep a business like this desperate. He didn't want to steal too much, avoiding infusing too much cash in the business through the insurance payout. He wanted the owners to need to take loans and lines of credit to keep the place afloat. This opened up the opportunity for loansharking with very high interest rates, or vigs, on the loan. Inevitably the owners can't make those payments, and the Family takes over the business using it for money laundering, continuing to overextend credit, and then re-selling goods until there is nothing left. The owners are then left with so much debt that they have to declare bankruptcy if they are fortunate enough not to be arrested for the crimes committed.

Johnny wasn't sure if this place was bankrolled or not. He decided to try his hand at talking up Nina, who didn't seem too comfortable talking to the public, to see what he could learn.

"You got some real nice stuff in here," Johnny stated after sauntering up behind Nina. A move designed to make her even more uncomfortable.

"Um, thanks," was Nina's simple reply, clearly startled by Johnny.

Johnny had already taken off his cap. He bent slightly to move himself into Nina's space, and rubbed his hand over his slicked back hair. "I'm sorry, I didn't mean to startle you," he said coolly.

"Oh no, you're fine," replied Nina, "I'm new at this gallery thing, so I'm sure it was just me."

"Really?" Johnny said smoothly, "I never would have thought that. You seem like you're in charge, to me anyways."

"Well thank you...," Nina started to reply until Johnny interrupted.

"Johnny, nice to meet you," he said while extending his hand which Nina shook quickly.

"So, you're interested in art?" Nina asked.

"Well, sorta. You see, I'm actually interested in the art gallery, more the business side of things, honestly Nina." Johnny replied, using some basic con methods like implanting the notion that he is honest in her mind before she can judge that he is not, and using her name to start a personal connection. He was an old pro at these techniques. Johnny was also taking a chance that Nina wasn't the artist. She was dressed conservatively in brown slacks, a blue blouse with a high collar that covered her neck, and heavy black shoes. She had dark rimmed glasses, and her hair was done in a stylish tightly wound bun. Her primary tell was that she never even hinted at any of the art when she welcomed people to the gallery.

Nina leaned in a little, bringing the back of her hand up against her mouth as if letting Johnny in on a little secret. "Honestly, Johnny, so am I. My partner Meya is the artist, I handle the business side." She seemed to stand a little straighter and more confidently, knowing that this was her area of expertise.

"I just wonder how a place like this makes money. I mean do you all have to pay for all this before you can hang it and sell it? That must be a lot of cash to come up with all at once," Johnny asked, holding his hat in both hands gently in front of himself.

"No, not exactly," Nina responded, "we have most of it on consignment, some that we just show but isn't for sale, and a few pieces that Meya's father procured for her to complete the gallery." *'So Daddy is bankrolling this',* Johnny estimated, knowing that meant there wasn't much opportunity for loan sharking or similar prospects.

"If I can ask, how much do you make on the consignment pieces?" Johnny asked gently.

"Not at all," replied Nina who was more than happy to talk to someone about the business side of things and something other than art. "We get 40% since we are a new gallery. Once we get established that will probably push to 50%, but 40% for now."

"And which pieces are on consignment?" Johnny continued.

"We have several," Nina said pointing to a piece hanging on the wall, "for example, this is a piece by an artist from the Berkshires in Massachusetts. She specializes in glass paintings that are created by dropping color onto hot glass plates. It gives the piece not only unique color contrasts and patterns, but also affects the surface of the piece providing added texture. It really is beautiful. Meya, of course, can tell you much more about the artist."

Johnny stopped and studied the piece, lowering his cap, which he still held in both hands, from his chest to his waist.

He leaned in slightly. The large piece was a base of blue hues, from deep to light, with contoured streaks of green, yellow, and tan. A calming piece, it reminded him of a decoration that he had seen on a desk that contained several colors of sand. When the decoration was moved, the sand shifted creating random swirling patterns. The piece he was studying was much more impressive and imposing though, but very tranquil. It made him feel like he was staring at the warm ocean at sunset the time his father took the family to Asbury Beach. *'Maybe this is what lookin' at art is supposed to be like?'*, he wondered to himself.

"It really is beautiful. So, what does something like this go for?" he asked.

"This piece is selling for $10,000," Nina replied without batting an eye. Johnny nearly dropped his hat.

"Wow, I didn't realize that something like this went for that much," Johnny said with genuine amazement.

"She is an established but more localized artist. The price will increase as her pieces start to sell and circulate, for sure," replied Nina.

"I really should be letting you get back to the other guests, but can I ask which pieces are the ones that you own that are for sale?"

"We own the two glass bowls located on the pedestals," Nina replied. "They are from an artist from the West coast, Christian Jayle. He studied under Chihuly, and actually did some work at the Corning Museum of Glass."

"Impressive," replied Johnny, "and for something like this?"

Nina handed Johnny a binder which contained photos of some of the pieces with artist information and prices, as she added "the paintings for sale are also listed in there. We also have some pieces that Meya painted displayed in the front part of the gallery," Nina added.

'*Wow*', Johnny thought to himself, '*these places are goldmines.*'

"Well, Nina, this place is very impressive. You must have some serious security to protect all of this nice stuff." Nina hesitated in responding to this statement. The line of questioning was starting to go a little farther than she was comfortable with.

Just then Meya walked in and joined them. "Meya!" Nina said, straightening her posture slightly, "you're back. How was the trip?"

"Not great, we aren't getting any more time, but we can talk more later," Meya replied.

"Um, ok. This is Johnny. We were just talking about one of Isha's pieces," Nina offered. She realized that she might have said too much to Johnny already, and didn't want to reveal that to Meya.

"Hello, I'm Johnny. It is a very beautiful piece," Johnny said introducing himself while turning his view towards the glass piece and then back to Nina and Meya. He could detect that Nina was different since Meya showed up, but didn't exactly understand their dynamic yet.

"Oh, are you a collector?', Meya asked hopefully.

"No, not me. Don't have the scratch for that, shall we say?" Johnny said with the kindest smile that he could muster. "Nina and I were more talking about the business side of things, weren't we Nina?" he asked, which made Nina start to squirm.

Johnny bailed her out by adding, "It's very impressive how well you both have done establishing this gallery, especially with being so young. Sorry, I don't mean to offend, but just saying." He was counting on Meya being a bit of an ego queen.

"No offense at all. Thank you. It has been a lot of work," she replied without missing a beat. Nina's shoulders relaxed slightly, relieved Meya didn't seem to focus on their conversation.

"Only one more thing and we're all set," Meya said, "the security system." Nina's eyes widened and mouth opened slightly as she snapped her head at Meya. She could not believe what Meya had just offered up. Nina tried to interrupt, "What she means is the upgrade to the security system. We have all the basics in place."

Johnny held up both hands in front of his chest while continuing to hold his cap in one. "Wait. Don't worry. I get it, and I can actually help you. See, I'm in the security system business. I have to come clean, Nina, I really came today to see if I could drum up a new client in your gallery. I noticed right away that there is no security system," Johnny offered. Nina shifted her weight on her feet, responding with a skeptical look. Meya did not change expression or posture at all. "I would be happy to help you all out. I can put in the works, just say the word. I'm all out of business cards, unfortunately, but I live in the neighborhood and would be at your beck and call 24/7...no problem. I can give you my number and you can think about it."

He could not believe what may be about to happen. *'They're gonna give me the keys to the kingdom.'* he thought, maintaining his poker face while he finished working the scam. Johnny provided his information, instructed them to call him day or night, thanked them, and then put on his hat and left.

"Can you believe this?" Meya asked excitedly. "This must be an omen. What luck! The other guys back out and this guy walks in with only a few weeks left before Father is going to shut us down. He gave us another month, by the way. That's why I had to go in person, so I could turn on the tears. It always gets to him."

"I don't know, Meya," Nina said in a doubting tone, "this guy asked a lot of questions and we don't really know anything about him."

"Look, we have to take a chance here. No one else is available, and he's from the neighborhood so we can find him if we need him. I want this place to work, Nina, and I don't want to risk Father shutting us down." Meya said firmly.

Nina knew that arguing was useless. "Ok. Why not? You're just going to do it anyway," Nina said relenting.

She had seen this behavior many times from Meya. Her impulsive changes in her majors, her fascination with Chad, even the time that she picked up her new convertible in red and decided hours later that it should be blue. She didn't even sleep on her decision, she just drove right back to the dealer and demanded a different car. She got it at Daddy's expense, of course. *'Whatever'*, thought Nina, *'her father is the one bankrolling this place, not me.'*

Meya dialed the phone. Johnny picked up almost immediately.

"Johnny, it's Meya. When can you start?"

15

Jake was working in the kitchen cleaning up after another day of serving the surprisingly regular pace of customers that came through the door. He was glad that things had stabilized at The Athena, but still couldn't understand how the place stayed in business. *'A question for another time'*, he thought.

Pedro had left for the evening, and Sarah was still working in the dining room. Jake stopped when he heard what seemed to be muffled male voices followed by the beep of the cash register opening. He knew that Sarah had cashed out earlier that evening, and was going to take the excess money to the night deposit drop at the bank when she left.

Jake moved to the swing door, opening it slightly and peeking out through the crack. He saw Sarah at the cash register, as he expected, but also two other men. One was large and young, and was standing just beside her. He wore a black tracksuit with a white stripe across the back of the jacket. His head was shaved and a gaudy gold chain hung around his thick neck. The other was older. He had a pointy nose, wore a flat cap, and was thin with dark hair slicked back. He was slowly and absent mindedly spinning the point of a small silver dagger into the table where he was seated.

Jake quickly surmised that the two men were robbing the place and didn't see Sarah as much of a threat. An immediate dread that any financial loss could be the tipping point causing him to lose the restaurant, and maybe even Sarah, shot through his mind. While things seemed calm, he wasn't willing to risk any harm coming to her once she had given them the money from the register. *'These guys aren't even wearing masks'*, Jake thought to himself, *'who knows if they're in the business of leaving witnesses?'*

Jake reached for the nearest weapon that he could find, a meat mallet. He had used the square, spiked head of the heavy instrument to hammer and flatten meat for some of the dishes. He now hoped that he could win with it against a knife, and even more challenging, against two men.

He also didn't care. Nothing was going to take Sarah away from him.

Jake quickly contemplated his next move: rush out to maximize the element of surprise, or enter slowly to try to close the distance before they noticed him. Opting for the latter, he slowly opened the door a little farther and took a few quiet steps out of the kitchen and into the dining room. After three steps, the man at the table noticed Jake wielding the meat mallet. "Hey, easy bud," he said after quickly surmising the situation.

His statement only acted as a starter pistol for Jake. He shot towards the man at the cash register like a tiger attacking its prey. As he was advancing, Sarah turned and shouted, "No, Jake!" but it was to no avail. Jake lunged at the bald man who was raising his arms to protect himself. As he landed on him, Jake started to swing the mallet at the man's bald head.

Sarah grabbed at Jake's swinging arm with both of her arms and all her strength, slowing it slightly and affecting his grip. Jake dropped his weapon, but his forearm struck the bald man, knocking him off balance. The bald man quickly caught his bearings, righting himself as he pushed Jake away. It was obvious to Jake that this wasn't the man's first altercation, but it didn't matter. Jake was in defense and attack mode at the same time.

Bald man grunted, "You're gonna pay for that," and swung a practiced haymaker towards Jake. Jake shifted to one side avoiding the powerful blow, but the punch struck Sarah's shoulder on the follow through, sending her skidding across the floor.

Jake felt the rage swell instantly. No one was going to hit Sarah again…ever.

Jake returned fire with a punch that was fueled by all of the pain, anger, fear, and love that was pent up in his being. The punch landed squarely on the bald man's nose, knocking him back hard against the counter, and dropping him immediately to his hands and knees on the floor.

"Alright, enough!" shouted the man in the cap. This plus the culmination of the fighting seemed to stop everything.

Jake looked at him for just a second, and then moved to Sarah. "Are you ok?" he asked. Sarah turned to Jake. There were no visible signs of injury, but he could see her eyes were wide and wild and she was shaking.

"What have you done, Jake?!" Sarah yelled, tears streaming down her cheek forming black streaks from her smeared eyeliner. "This is so bad!" she wailed as she slammed her palms into the floor.

"Your missus got that right," the man with the cap said. "You can bet we'll be back," he continued as he helped the bald man to his feet and towards the door, "and next time the visit won't be nearly as pleasant."

16

"What the hell did you two do?!" Zehab yelled as he entered the restaurant like a snorting bull, again startling the few customers. "Kitchen now!" he demanded of Sarah. When he entered the kitchen he immediately ordered Pedro out, "Cover the front, I have to talk to these two fools." Sarah and Pedro nearly ran into each other as they changed rooms.

Following the altercation, once she had calmed down, Sarah had explained to Jake what was actually happening. The two men were members of the local Mafia and were collecting their weekly contribution to the 'Neighborhood Watch' part of their extortion racket.

"I didn't know," Jake offered before Zehab could start. "Didn't know?...didn't know? That is your excuse? Didn't know?!, Zehab asked in disbelief. "How could you not know? Everyone in this neighborhood knows," he continued.

"I never told him," Sarah added, trying to protect Jake, "he was just trying to protect me...protect the restaurant."

"Well that you did not do," Zehab responded. "Let me tell you what you did do. You have sealed not only the restaurant's fate, but your fate as well. If we are lucky all that they will do is keep customers from coming here until they finish with you. Maybe then they will let us open again. I am sure that we will have to pay more, of course. And we will be watched constantly to see if there is any other way that they can use The Athena for their business. Who knows what that will be? It will probably just be a slow death no matter what...and that is the best case." He was referring to the fate of the restaurant, but Jake wasn't so sure that it didn't also apply to him.

"As for you," he continued talking directly to Jake, "you almost broke the one that they call 'Nicky Scars' nose. He isn't going to forget that. They will come for you, and if they can't find you they will find *her*," he emphasized while pointing at Sarah.

A feeling of disbelief washed over Jake. This couldn't be happening. He couldn't be losing what he cared about again. The old sinking feelings closed in. He felt a sudden pressure in the middle of his mind and a heaviness in his chest that he knew all too well from his past. His father...Red...now Sarah. All that he could think was *'not again'* over and over.

"He has skills!" Sarah called out suddenly. "Can't you talk to them? Maybe work something out...anything?"

"No, I am sure that they will not listen. These are men of violence, not reason. They will not listen," Zehab responded while he rubbed his chin as he tried to figure out some sort of solution to save his business.

Zehab needed The Athena. The business was not at all profitable, but that wasn't the point for him. The scheming opportunist Zehab used the business as a front to take extended loans and lines of credit to use for his other business ventures. In response he piled debt onto The Athena books, using it as a way to reduce the taxes he actually paid. His business model was a continuous shell game of moving money from venture to venture, driving investment and then gradually failing on all fronts and under all sorts of LLCs. All of this while he managed to skim a nice portion for his personal use.

"Maybe he can cook for them, or do odd jobs or something else that he knows how to do. You can tell them all that he has done for you. Maybe they will find that type of service valuable," Sarah pleaded. "Can't you at least try?" she begged. The thought of losing Jake was evidently wrenching at her emotions as well.

"I can try to talk to them. I do not think it will work, but maybe it will lessen the pain that is surely coming like a storm," Zehab replied. Saying it out loud did not further convince him. "They are located across the street at the delicatessen. Make your best dish and I will take it over with our best wine. Then we will have to see," Zehab instructed, "and it must be soon before the retaliation comes."

Without a word Jake sped off to start cooking. Sarah thanked Zehab and followed him.

Soon Jake would find out if it would again be time to leave, for both he and Sarah.

17

"I think I got something boss," Johnny said excitedly as he walked into the back of the delicatessen where Sonny was sitting and talking with Archie and Dominic.

"I told you to use protection!" Sonny joked, laughing boisterously as he rose and put his arm around Johnny's shoulder. "Stupid mook. C'mon let's go get you some cream or shit for your junk," he continued boisterously. Dominic laughed along with Sonny's childish joke. Archie only smiled slightly without changing position in his chair.

Sonny led Johnny outside. "What the frig is wrong with you?" he said while squaring himself to Johnny. "Sei stupido? You're going to get us knocked down if you ain't careful."

"Sorry Boss. I wasn't thinking," Johnny apologized, "but I think that I got something good. Louie put me on to it," he continued, trying to shift Sonny's focus off his screw up.

"Let's hear it, genius," Sonney replied, working a toothpick from one side of his mouth to the other as they started to walk.

Johnny first covered his mouth with his hand, a habit that they had formed to keep prying eyes, in particular the Feds, from picking up what they were saying with surveillance. Then he started to fill Johnny in on what he found. "There's a new art gallery in the old phone company building. Fancy place being run by two girls from out of town. Seem to be barely out of high school, fugget about it. Anyways, I was talking to one of them and I estimate that there is probably fifty to a hundred thousand hanging on those walls."

"Yeah?" Sonny said, raising his eyebrows at the big dollar amount.

"Wait, you ain't heard the best part. There's no security system."

Sonny stopped walking and looked at Johnny skeptically. Covering his mouth by shifting his toothpick with his hand he said, "You sure? No security system with all of the money hanging on the wall?"

"Yeah," Johnny continued, "but that still ain't the best part."

"Oh, this I gotta hear," Sonny replied.

"They are hiring *us* to install their system," Johnny stated.

This statement hung in the air for a second. "Us?" Sonny confirmed.

"Us," replied Johnny.

"How exactly did you manage that?" Sonny asked.

"I told you…young, inexperienced. I feel like they had some kind of deadline or something. I couldn't believe our luck. We set the system, we beat the system."

"We walk with a hundred thousand," Sonny finished his sentence. Sonny was sure the money and the creative score would make the other families notice, notice at least he and his crew and their potential.

"Who do we know in the alarm business?" Sonny asked Johnny.

"We know Sean O'Connel, but he got pinched for trying to pull off pretty much what we are trying, just at an electronics store. Even though he's out, the cops are keeping an eye on him and all of his guys, but they're laying low and playing it straight for now."

"That may be a problem," Sonny surmised, "but a problem for another day. We're gonna make this score work," Sonny continued without giving Johnny any credit, his usual behavior. "We gotta find someone to fence the stuff too. I think that Arch has a guy. Probably gonna cost us, though. That prick hates me, I think."

"What about the old man?" Johnny asked, referring to Silvio. He was sure that Sonny's grandfather would not approve.

Sonny thought on this while they walked. "I'll bring it to Arch. Ask him what he thinks. Keeps us in line but off the radar if he thinks it is a bad idea. We'll deal with the next step after that. A hundred grand might be enough scratch to shake him loose."

The men made their way back to the delicatessen. Sonny knew that he was walking a razors edge. He had pledged loyalty to the family at his induction ceremony, swearing to 'live and die' by the gun and knife that were laid out on the table in front of him at his ceremony to become a made Mafia guy. His trigger finger was then pricked with a pin, blood trickling onto a holy card that was then set on fire. Sonny could still feel the heat and burning on his palms as he passed the flaming card back and forth while swearing that he would burn in Hell if he betrayed any member of the family. While the ceremony was still vivid in his mind, the knowledge that the ritual likely meant more to his grandfather than himself was as well.

Conversely, he wanted to make a name for himself in the larger organization and command the respect and power he felt he deserved and obsessively desired. Even so, he still felt an obligation to his grandfather to bring this opportunity forward.

Sonny and Johnny walked into the back of the delicatessen to talk to Archie, who was now alone. "Arch, you got a minute. I think that we got something good and want your council."

Archie looked up from his newspaper at the two of them. He was already skeptical, but held his poker face, "Sure kid. Whatcha got?"

"So, we cased a new art gallery in the old phone building," he said, again taking credit for his crew's work. "A lot of money in there, Johnny says."

"Probably a hundred thousand, maybe more," Johnny added. Sonny shot Johnny a quick look. Johnny instantly receded, knowing that he had spoken out of turn.

"Yeah, so anyway," Sonny started again, turning back to Archie whose slight smirk drifted back to his poker face, "pretty good scratch, but that isn't even the best part. Two girls are running the place that don't seem to have any idea how to run a business. They even hired this giamoke," using his middle finger to point at Johnny, "to install the security system, if you can freakin' believe it."

Archie's eyebrows raised at this statement, which both Sonny and Johnny queued in on immediately. "Right, fugget about it," Sonny commented, nodding. "So all that we need is for one of Sean's guys to handle the install of the system and we can pick the place clean. We can use your guy to fence the stuff, with a healthy cut for you of course."

Archie thought on this for a second, eyeing up first Sonny and then Johnny. "That's a good find, I will say that," he started. "One problem is that using Sean's guys ain't a good idea right now, cops will be all over it. A quick lift will get pinched as soon as we start. No good." Before Sonny could interrupt he continued, "Second problem is that Silvio will never go for it." Archie knew that Sonny knew this was the case and was just feeling him out to see if there was some possibility of it happening. He was surprised the kid came to him at all, but figured he was just looking for cover with Silvio. "Maybe you could put the system in place, pinch a couple of things and work the protection racket. Probably the safe play. The boss will approve that. He'll be real happy with you two as well."

The last part of this lecture really stung at Sonny's desires. *'Proud of me like I brought a good report card home'*, he thought, *'bullshit answer'*. "But we can't wait that long," Sonny argued, "the place may be shut down in a few months according to Johnny." Sonny was happy to pull Johnny in as the source of the information now that it sounded like the job was going to fall through. "Not enough time to make the protection racket work."

"Sounds like you need to leave this one alone then," Archie said, picking his paper up again.

The consultation was over. "Yeah, thanks Arch," Sonny replied. He and Johnny left.

Archie lowered his paper as they left, watching the door close behind them. He knew they were never going to leave it alone. Sonny had made a habit of finding his way into trouble fueled by his big ego and near constant pushing to move outside of the boss's rules. Archie knew about the time Sonny reached out to one of the cappos in a major family, looking to see if there were any opportunities for him. He was sent away as a liability based on reputation. Word made its way back to Archie. He intervened with Sonny and kept it from his grandfather to save the old man more pain over his grandson. Sonny, of course, just said that he was looking for new opportunities. "You know you don't go to another family without us knowing. Next time we better know first," Archie had scolded, "or your grandfather finds out for sure." His point had been made.

Archie also suspected that Sonny dabbled in drugs on the side, his crew selling some to make up his earnings when he needed to. Archie had never seen it himself, or had a trusted associate verify, so no action was taken. Even still it was against the boss's orders and opened the family up to extended prison sentences and liability. And then there was the time that Sonny disrespected a made guy in another family. That one still haunted the Amoretti family.

'*No way this is over*', he thought to himself, before starting to contemplate Sonny's next move.

18

Jake laid on the worn bed in his room at the Elm Inn staring absently at the ceiling. His mind was focusing on a fate that was completely out of his hands. He didn't hear the music from the next room passing easily through the thin, uninsulated walls. He didn't hear Joe when he walked past the door to Jake's room, again in boisterous conversation with one of the voices in his head. Playing through the possible scenarios of Zehab's meeting with the Mafia engulfed Jake's full attention.

After considering a particularly gruesome outcome Jake snapped out of his trance, allowing some other emotions to enter his consciousness. He realized what he wanted more than anything at that moment was to talk to Red. Jake had spoken to his mother again a few days earlier and found out Red had been discharged from the hospital and moved to a rehab facility. Jake went to the payphone in the lobby and dialed the number.

"Apple Rehab," a woman's voice said spiritedly after two rings.

"Hi. Um, Red Miller's room please," Jake responded, feeling strange having never really used Red's last name before.

"Sure, one second," the woman responded, followed by a click as he was put on hold. After a long pause she came back on the line, "I'm sorry, he is in occupational therapy right now. Can I take a message?"

Jake was crestfallen he wasn't going to be able to talk to Red. He longed for his mentorship in his time of crisis as Red had provided in the past. "Sure, just tell him that Jake called, thanks," Jake responded solemnly, preparing to hang up.

"Did you say Jake?" the woman asked.

"Um, yeah, I'm Jake," Jake responded.

"Are you *the* Jake, the Jake he talks about all of the time? The one from the scout camp?" she continued inquiring.

Jake's curiosity piqued, and he felt a slight feeling of anticipation starting to build in his chest. "That's me, am I in trouble or something?" he asked.

The woman on the other end laughed at his response. "Heavens no, you're not in trouble," she responded, "but I do have something to read to you."

Jake's was now wholly engaged. The woman continued, "He left a note for you in case you called with strict instructions to read it verbatim…word for word, and we shouldn't try to summarize it or screw it up with any of our own fluff. Your friend Red can be real ornery when he wants to."

"You don't have to tell me," Jake responded jokingly, his mood already lifting with memories of his time with Red, "so what does the ornery guy have to say?"

The woman began to relay Red's words…

Hey Jake. Wasn't sure if you were going to call or not, so I figured I would leave you a message in case I wasn't able to talk. They have me doing all kinds of things here so I never know when I'll be free. First, I'm alive. Gonna take more than an explosion to take me out. Second, I'm still kicking. More figuratively than actually, but I'm getting there.

Third, you do what you need to do, and don't worry about me. Call your mom to make sure she knows you're ok, but don't stop doing what you need to do. This is your thing, don't let others tell you how to do it. Also, don't let the city get you. It can be a tricky place. Stay true to yourself, keep your eyes open, and stay focused on finding what you need to move on. I'll be here if you need me, but you don't. You got this.

Finally, you better be taking care of that motorcycle. You pawn it for some crotch rocket, and you and me are going to have a problem. Well, I better finish this before nurse Cratchit comes collecting me for the next physical therapy torture session.

Take care of yourself,
Red

"That's all of it, Jake, word for word," the woman finished up.

Jake, with tears running down his cheeks could only muster a weak, "Thanks, tell him I called, ok".

"Sure will hon. You take care of yourself and we'll take care of him. Don't worry, we've dealt with people ornerier than him. Goodbye Jake," and the woman hung up.

Jake tried to process every word that he could remember from Red's message. *'I did try to stay true to myself by protecting Sarah, but look where it got me'*, he thought. Even so, Jake took refuge in the fact that Red was still covering all of the basis, even from afar. *'Nothing is going to kill him, even an explosion'*, he thought, shaking his head in amazement.

"Well, Red, I hope that an explosion isn't waiting for me."

19

Zehab crossed the street from The Athena to the delicatessen carrying the warm dish of moussaka and a bottle of wine. He bypassed the front entrance and walked around the corner to the alley behind the business. The back door was gray and all metal, reinforced with heavy bolts around the perimeter and dented in several spots. A few different colors of paint were revealed in the layers evident in a deep scratch in one of the dents. The only other feature besides the worn knob and deadbolt was a small sliding window. He knocked and waited nervously. After a pause, the small sliding window slid open.

Zehab could see a large eye and the top of a bandage on a man's nose through the window. "Yeah?" the deep voice on the other side of the door asked.

"I'm Zehab from The Athena. Apparently there was a misunderstanding the other night. I am coming to apologize and try to reconcile the situation." He knew not to say more through the door, and again waited.

The window slid shut. After a long minute Zehab could hear the deadbolt being unlatched and the door opening. A hulking man who Zehab knew as Nicky Scars opened the door. He said nothing, but looked at Zehab with enough of a menacing look that Zehab's nervousness grew three-fold. Trying to keep his cool, Zehab entered the back room of the delicatessen.

His attempt to maintain a poker face was betrayed by his intense sweating and short breaths. "Come in. Sounds like you have a problem, friend," a different gangster sitting at a table said. "I believe one of your employees chose not to honor our agreement and took it out on my guys," he continued. Based on his questions Zehab quickly surmised that he was the boss of the crew. Zehab knew Johnny and Nicky because they were the ones who collected payment, and had seen the lead gangster before but had never met him.

Zehab decided to try speaking first, "I am very sorry. He is a new worker. He didn't know."

"Where was your cousin?" Johnny interrupted.

"Cousin?" the gangster who seemed to be in charge asked.

"Yeah, Deniz, I told you about him Sonny. He is who usually makes our payment." Sonny nodded and turned back to Zehab. "Instead, it was the girl and that idiot," Johnny continued, "so, where was he?"

"We had a disagreement. He won't be around anymore," Zehab answered.

"Too bad, he kept you out of trouble, which you most definitely are in, my friend," Sonny added sarcastically.

"I know, and for that I am sorry. It will never happen again. I bring moussaka and wine for you all to enjoy...as a peace offering...please." He laid the tray and set the bottle on the table in front of Sonny.

"It's going to take a lot more than some food and wine to fix this. This won't even cover Nicky's nose, huh Scars?" Sonny said, turning to Nicky. Nicky didn't move. He just deepened his threatening stare at Zehab.

"Of course, I understand," Zehab said as he laid an envelope fat with cash on top of the tray of food. "I hope that this helps with Nicky's nose."

Zehab could feel Nicky's rage fill the room. Sonny, however, roared with laughter. "You got balls, I'll give you that. You know it's all I can do to keep Nicky from tearing your guy in half," Sonny said through his laughter. Johnny stared motionless at Zehab.

Sonny continued, "Well, this, plus paying double each time, might make you and your business right with us." Johnny especially didn't approve of this arrangement, but knew there was no negotiation with Sonny. "But you will have to give us the kid."

"Jake? I can't do that. Without my cousin I need him to cook. My business will close," Zehab responded.

"That sounds like a *you* problem, not a *me* problem, as my niece likes to say, spoiled little bitch," Sonny said, leaning forward in his chair and pointing at Zehab for emphasis.

Zehab started to sweat even more, but quickly replied, "Actually, with all due respect, it is a *you* problem as well."

"What did you say to me?" Sonny asked, rising from his chair. Zehab could sense Nicky taking a step towards him.

"Listen to me, please," Zehab pleaded, "if I close then you lose your double payments, and some fancy brand will probably move in. We both know that corporations are much less likely to pay anything for protection. I am a sure thing if you keep me open."

Sonny sat down again contemplating this position. "That's true boss," Johnny commented. Sonny didn't break his contemplation.

"Well, there has to be some retribution against this 'Jake'. It don't look too good to our other customers if this guy can walk with nothing. You got another envelope of money in your other pocket, or maybe we should go into business with you, how about that?" Sonny asked.

"I don't have more money, but I do have something else to offer," Zehab responded.

He couldn't believe that he was about to offer Jake's services as retribution. '*Things are about to go from bad to worse*', he thought, but he really didn't have any other choice. He had to try to maintain control of The Athena. "The kid, Jake, has skills," he continued before they could respond. "Not just cooking, he can do plumbing and wiring. That kind of stuff. He's done it at the restaurant."

Sonny started to sit back and laugh in disbelief, but Johnny interrupted his theatrics with a question, "Did you say he knows wiring and stuff?"

"Yeah," Zehab said perking up, hoping that he might have actually found a bargaining chip, "he has fixed two outlets, replaced the temperature gauge on the freezer, and fixed one of the fans on the range. He knew what to get, bought it, and fixed it. And it all works."

"What are you thinking, Johnny?" Sonny asked. He had worked with Johnny long enough to tell when he was on to something.

"I'm thinking that maybe this kid could solve our O'Connel problem," Johnny offered. Sonny took just a second to process this, and a large smile grew across his face as the thought clicked.

"Well, Za-hat...or whatever your name is, you just might have gotten lucky. Bring the kid over."

"It's Zehab, and I will go and get him," Zehab replied. He stood and was escorted to the door by the still seething Nicky.

"You really think this might work?" Sonny asked.

"I don't give a shit if it will work or not, that little prick broke my nose. It's my turn to destroy his!" Nicky exclaimed.

Sonny turned to Nicky and said calmly, "Was I talking to you?" Pausing for effect he continued, "No, I wasn't. I know you want to end him, but he could be the key to a lot of money. Now, after we finish the job…that's a different story. He's all yours." Nicky wasn't thrilled with this response, but understood. That would be the end of the conversation.

Sonny turned back to Johnny, raising his eyebrows and moving his head slightly in a sarcastic 'Well, I'm waiting for your answer' motion. "Maybe. The system that I spoke to Sean about is all wired. Not complicated, he says, if you know a little about how to do wiring and have an ounce of common sense. Let's see what the kids got, get into him a little and see how he handles it. I got ideas," Johnny replied.

"You always do, luckily for us," Sonny said, now the consummate team player since it benefited him.

Zehab returned quickly with Jake. He filled him in a little bit, telling him they may need some wiring work and that just might save his life, amazingly. Zehab knocked on the door and Nicky opened it forcefully without even peering through the small window. He glared at Jake, who would have run except his legs were temporarily paralyzed with fear. "Nic, let'm in," Sonny shouted, and Nicky moved slightly to the side, never once taking his gaze from Jake.

Zehab started to walk in, but Jake stood frozen. "What are you doing? Stop being a coward. Move," Zehab commanded, grabbing Jake's sleeve and pulling him into the room. They made their way to Sonny and Johnny.

"So, you're Jake. Maybe I should call you 'slugger' instead, what do you think Nic?" Sonny said, breaking into laughter. No one else laughed, especially Nicky whose glare only turned more threatening as he clenched both hands into tight fists. "So, Zehat tells me that you're good with wiring and shit. That true?"

"Yeah, I do wiring repair," Jake answered.

"Wiring repair, where'd you learn that?" Sonny asked.

"I worked at a scout camp back home fixing stuff," Jake said as bravely as he could muster despite being very nervous, "Red taught me to do that and other stuff."

"Who's Red and why do I care?" asked Sonny crassly.

Jake hadn't even realized that he said Red's name. Trying to recover he clarified as steadily as he could muster, "He was the caretaker at the camp. I just worked for him. It doesn't matter."

"We could use some repair over here, in fact. How about fixing that light over the poker table?" Sonny more directed than asked.

Jake turned to look at the fixture. It was a hanging lamp with a green glass shade and a single bare bulb. The shade was coated with years of dust. Realizing that he had no real choice, Jake replied, "Sure, let me go and get my tools and I'll be right back." Jake started to turn towards the door.

"How about you fix it now," Sonny said in a stone cold tone, "and if it doesn't work when you're done I may have to turn Nicky loose on you."

Jake started to sweat as a streak of fear shot through him. So many variables could be entirely out of his control. Bad switch, faulty light socket, chewed through wire in the wall, and several other things all flashed through his brain at once. Knowing that he really didn't have any choice, his reply was simple, "ok."

A worn octagon shaped poker table sat in the corner. The felt was threadbare and stained. The varnish was worn in front of four of the spaces, telling Jake that usually only four people played. Dark black bar chairs with vinyl padding sat at each of these spots. Above the table was the broken hanging lamp.

"Which switch?" Jake asked.

Johnny pointed to a double gang switch plate on the wall. "The right one," he said as he pointed. Jake made his way over to the switch and cycled it a few times. The light did not illuminate, as expected. He cycled the other switch which turned on another light in the room, confirming that the issue was likely not a blown fuse. He next removed the bulb from the lamp, and shook it gently to verify that the filament was not broken. He moved to the socket housing in the lamp. He verified that the wires looked connected properly. Jake realized that an issue with the switch was the only other possibility that would be in his control to fix at that moment.

He took the Swiss army knife that his father had given him from his pocket, and then used the screwdriver to remove the switch plate. Under the plate was dusty and dark. He again cycled the switch with the same result as before. He next started to unscrew the long screws that held the switch into the electrical box in the wall. This was his last option, and he had to calm himself down to be able to properly work the tool. Sonny, Johnny, Zehab, and Nicky were all watching him work. Nicky was paying especially close attention, hoping that he would fail so that he could provide his own special consequence.

Jake wiped his brow with his sleeve and began to unscrew the switch screws. When the screws were about halfway out, Jake pulled at the switch to start to straighten the packed wires. Miraculously, one of the wires sparked briefly and the light flickered. Jake realized instantly that the wire that provides power to the switch had come loose slightly with the years of cycling, dust, and temperature changes. Although not very safe, Jake removed the live switch, turned the switch off, and then carefully re-attached the wire. When he was finished he turned the switch on and the light blazed to life. Jake could audibly hear Zehab breathe a sigh of relief, and could sense Nicky's disappointment. Jake felt his own breathing calm slightly as well.

"Hey, you did it," Sonny said, pleased not only that Jake had been able to fix it, but also that he had been able to keep his cool and focus while doing so.

"You think that you could install a wired security system?" Johnny asked immediately, knowing that Jake had passed Sonny's test.

Jake pondered this for a second thinking about the cabin rewire that he and Red had completed on cabin four. "Yeah, I could do that," he said with as much confidence as he could muster.

"That's good," Sonny said, "because your life and the life of that little girlfriend of yours depends on it."

20

"You ready to go?" Johnny asked.

"As ready as I can be, I think," Jake replied.

"You *think* you're ready? I am not sure you yet understand the gravity of this. You don't want to screw it up, you got me?" Sonny interjected.

"I'm ready," Jake replied as resolutely as he could muster.

"Now, that's more like it," Sonny said evenly.

Even though he wasn't doing the actual installation, Sean O'Connel had set them up with a system. He was promised a cut of the job, and knew that there would be more jobs to follow if this worked. He was impressed with Jake's basic understanding of electrical systems and ability to work with his hands. Under different circumstances he might have considered Jake for his crew, assuming he could trust him. He knew Jake was doing this under duress, but he didn't know why, which was just fine with him. The less he knew the better.

Sean had provided a basic system with door alarms, several pressure sensors for some of the more expensive paintings, and four cameras with monitors. In the most modern museum they would also include a more sophisticated laser motion network or other newer technology, but the gallery didn't really call for that. In reality, this system would prove only marginally effective even if the installation was legitimate since there was no armed guard response on the property. A professional art thief who did their homework could be in and out of the gallery stealing the desired pieces in minutes, long before the police would respond. Even so, this type of system was applicable to this type of gallery, making the owners and exhibited artists more comfortable. It also checked an important box for the company insuring the gallery.

The system was wired and looked complex. Nina had managed to convince Meya to ask a few more questions before finally agreeing to the install. Johnny fielded them like a pro. He explained 'multi-level gallery security model', a term that he entirely made up, referring to the combination of the perimeter entry alarms, pressure sensors, and cameras. He also headed off concerns that the technology for a wireless system was too new and easier to hack, emphasizing that a professionally installed, wired system is the best way to go. He finally sealed it by promising to be there in two days, understanding that they are under a time crunch that no other company would meet, even mail order, do-it-yourself.

This seemed to bolster Meya's belief in her original decision. Without even following up with Nina she agreed to it all. "See you in two days".

Jake and Sean strapped all of the equipment onto a rolling cart and loaded it into the white nondescript cargo van that Johnny had borrowed from an associate. Johnny drove, and they headed to the gallery. Jake was as prepared as he could be short of doing an actual installation beforehand. He was even dressed to fit the part in Dickie brand work pants and a buttoned work shirt.

Meya was the only person at the gallery when Johnny walked in with Jake in tow pulling the equipment cart. "Hello Meya," Johnny said with his best smile, "this is Jake, he will be handling the installation."

Jake extended a hand to shake Meya's, offering only a simple, "Hello".

Meya had closed the gallery for the installation, and wanted to be sure of the duration. "About how long will the installation take?" she asked Jake.

"Should only be a few hours, I just have to grab my ladder from the van and I will get started right away," Jake replied.

"Great," Meya said, "I have a dinner appointment so that should be fine."

"Ok, sounds like we are all set. Meya, you have any questions or problems, you call me directly. You have my number," Johnny interjected while lightly clapping his hands together in front of his chest, "you are in good hands with Jake, he is our best installer." Jake masked his apprehension at Johnny's comment as best he could.

"I'm sure that we will be fine," Meya responded, her mind evidently already on to her next thought.

Jake walked out with Johnny to get the ladder. After retrieving it, Jake stopped at the driver's side window for any final advice from Johnny. "My advice…you really, really don't want to screw this up," he said as he drove off.

Jake returned to the gallery and got started. He took out all of the pieces and laid them at their respective locations within the gallery. He located two cameras and a wide motion sensor in the corner of the gallery, as well as one in the near corner with a view of the main door to cover the main exhibit space. He also planned to put a camera and motion sensor in the back to cover the storage area and back door. Pressure switches were located under five paintings along the outer two walls, and proximity switches were added to each door. All of the cameras were fed to a monitor in the office. He next installed entryway keypads at each door, and Meya insisted that they stick with the old keylock setup to maintain the aesthetics of the place, further convinced by Johnny that the rest of the system would provide more than adequate coverage. A single keypad was added inside the back door that activated and deactivated the system. The model that Sean selected conveniently had a secret override code as well.

Meya would occasionally ask Jake if he needed anything as he continued to lay out cable and started to install the components. She didn't stop to talk much and Jake didn't push it. The less she remembered about him the better. They worked in silence for most of the time, Meya addressing her work, or the internet on her computer as Jake noticed several times, and he, on the installation.

Even though he knew what was at stake if the installation went wrong, performing the installation in the brightly lit, climate controlled space surrounded by the beautiful art was actually very calming for Jake. He always loved the logic of this type of work. The way that the elements of the system each had a function and purpose, and always carried out that function when harmonized together in the final installation. Even the troubleshooting that came with every job was a logical step-by-step puzzle ready to be solved through systematic dissection. The only real emotion that came with this type of work was fatigue after a hard day's work, frustration which was usually limited for Jake with his skill, and satisfaction at the final result. He found power in his ability to work with his hands, to repair the broken, and build something from nothing…even if it was for the Mafia.

As the day wore on, shadows caused by the late afternoon sun began to form in the gallery. It gave Jake an even stronger appreciation for the talent of the artists as the shadows and red tones from the fading sunlight gave even greater depth to the pieces. Jake had finished the entire installation which was now operating perfectly. He had activated the system and even tripped it as a test. Right as designed it dialed directly to the phone that Johnny had set up specifically for this use. "Sounds like you pulled it off. Not sure if it's your best work or not, but it's probably your most important. Wrap things up and I'll bring the van in 15 minutes to collect you and the remaining stuff," Johnny offered.

Jake could feel the relief in his chest. Even though he had not realized it throughout the day, the successful installation felt like a ton of weight had been lifted from him. He would not die, nor would Sarah. He had done his part. They were free.

Not wasting any time, Jake cleaned up the pieces of cut wire, swept any dust from the install, and collected his tools and empty boxes strapping them on the cart. "I'm all set," he called to Meya, "I'm just going to run this downstairs with the ladder and I'll be right back to show you how to set the security code. After returning he showed Meya where each of the components was located, how to view the cameras on the display, and most importantly how to enter the security code on the keypad. Meya paid attention as best she could, and seemed satisfied at being able to arm and disarm the system with the code.

Before Jake could leave, she jumped up, grabbing her phone and punching a few keys. Jake watched her with a bit of bewilderment at the sudden flurry of activity. Before he could interrupt her to tell her he was leaving he heard her say, "Daddy, we did it. The security system is installed. The installer just finished…yes, just now…cameras, motion sensors, something for the paintings and a keypad with a security code." Jake didn't bother to provide her with the correct terminology. "It goes directly to the security company," she continued, now evidently answering questions, "the name of the company? Uh..." She looked at Jake with desperation in her eyes looking for the name. The name that Jake did not have. They had never established a name.

He thought quickly, hoping that Johnny hadn't already provided one. "Grove Security," he blurted out.

"Grove Security," Meya quickly said, "they're local Daddy, you can talk to the guy if you want to."

Jake's heart skipped a beat. He just wanted to finish the install and move on. This wasn't part of the plan. "Ok, I understand. Good luck with your meeting, Daddy. I love you too, and thanks Daddy," Meya said into the phone with a growing smile on her face. "Yes!" she exclaimed as she hung up pumping her fists in the air. "We did it," she continued as she threw her arms around Jake's neck, hugging him in celebration.

This took Jake aback momentarily, but he felt like celebrating as well, "Yes, we did. Never seen anyone so happy to have a security system," he joked.

Meya laughed as she released Jake. "Both my father and Chad are so focused on the security system. My father I get, but Chad's version of security is the black lock box in his office. Can you believe that's where he put the limited edition Jane Eyre I gave him for Christmas?"

"Jane Eyre?" Jake asked, never hearing of the book.

"Oh yes, it's a classic. All about the love between an older man and a younger woman." Jake smiled politely but was ready for the conversation, and the uncomfortable change in topic, to be over. "Anyway, I did it! This place is going to be great!" Meya exclaimed.

"Nina!" Meya suddenly shouted joyously, "we did it." Meya skirted past Jake who turned and saw her embrace another woman. As she released her bear hug, Meya introduced Jake, "this guy just finished installing the security system. I called my father and he is as happy as he gets. We are in the clear!" Nina shifted her attention to Jake. "This is Jake," Meya said, introducing him.

A sudden realization shot through Jake, the realization that he might have just ruined everything.

"Jake," said Nina, "I feel like we've met."

21

"I think Nina remembers me," Jake blurted to Johnny as he got into the passenger seat.

"What did you say?" Johnny asked to make sure he had heard Jake correctly.

"I met Nina at the open house. I went with Sarah. We talked to her for a while," Jake said with a sullen expression.

"Why the hell didn't you tell me that?" Johnny scolded.

"I just didn't think of it," Jake replied, crestfallen.

"You dumb mook, you've jeopardized this entire thing. Damnit! Things are gonna to be real bad when Sonny hears this."

They drove the few blocks in silence. Johnny was seething, but fortunately did some of his best scheming under pressure. When they got to the delicatessen Johnny instructed Jake to unload the truck and not say a thing about this to anyone. "I need some time to think," Johnny said as he continued to focus on how to avert the potential disaster.

Johnny walked to the back of the van and lit a cigarette while Jake unloaded it. Johnny recalled Nina's discomfort with using them for the security system. Recognizing Jake could ruin everything he had to find a way to prove that the system was sound, that the system worked. He needed to put her in a position where she doubted her intuition just enough. He rolled ideas over and over in his mind. He couldn't just magically make a robbery happen, and even if it did, keep the women from calling the police or Meya's father who might be more suspicious of the system.

As he kicked at the dirt finishing his smoke the idea hit him. He didn't need to stop an actual robbery, he just needed them to think that the system had stopped an actual robbery, and that the cops had shown up to arrest the thief.

Johnny flicked his cigarette butt to the ground and headed straight for the backroom. This was going to take some coordination and convincing, but that was what he did best.

Johnny and Jake entered the back room. Fortunately, only Sonny and Louie were there, waiting to hear how the installation went. "Well, does he live or die?" Sonny asked Johnny with little change in emotion, as if the question carried no more weight than any other part of their scam.

"The system is installed and works," Johnny replied.

"Excellent," Sonny said sitting back and looking at Jake who had entered after Johnny, "you get to live another day, boy scout."

"There is a small problem though," Johnny added. Sonny's disposition changed almost instantly. Louie listened intently. Johnny continued before Sonny could blow his top, "he thinks that one of the girls made him."

"What in the holy hell do you mean she made him? Where did she even see him?" Sonny asked, growing angrier.

"Sonny, that doesn't matter, I have a plan but we have to act fast. Does Sammy still have those police windbreakers that we got from that bought cop?" He was referring to the blue blazers with POLICE in large yellow letters on the back and the print of a badge on the front lapel. The question and the fact that Johnny seemed to have a solution brought Sonny back from the brink of violently attacking Jake. Louie's eyebrows raised with curiosity.

"Yeah, I think so," Sonny replied.

111

"Good, I'll reach out because we need those. Streets, we're gonna need you too."

*   *   *

It had only been a few days since the installation. Meya had not called, but Johnny had noticed that there was a van from another security service parked in the back of the building. It could have been for some other business, but Johnny knew that it could very well be Nina switching out the system at the gallery. Not taking any chances, Johnny sent his girlfriend to the gallery during the day to scope things out. She came back with photos of the cameras and motion detectors just as Johnny had installed them. *'A good sign'*, thought Johnny, *'but not a sure sign.'* He knew that they had to put the plan for the fake robbery into action that night.

After dark, Louie made his way to the back of the building. Streetwise and experienced, he bypassed the back door and instead made his way up the fire escape. He climbed to the floor above the gallery. Johnny's girlfriend had left the window unlatched next to the fire door, allowing quick, easy access for him. He was careful to lock the window after he entered.

Louie next made his way to the back entrance of the gallery. A skilled lockpick from days past he inserted his picking tools into the lock on the steel door. He worked the tools back and forth gliding them along the pins of the old lock, aligning each based on feel until, after several minutes, the lock rotated. He slowly opened the door to avoid making too much noise, using a headlamp to light his way into the gallery. The main space was illuminated by the streetlamps and other lights in the city, making the headlamp almost unnecessary. Even so, he used one as instructed.

He purposely scanned the small storage room and office, then made his way to the main gallery. He walked to a medium sized painting that looked like a dense fog with only shapes in the background. *'I'll never understand, who the hell would pay money for this?'*, he wondered to himself, while removing the painting from the wall. He next lifted one of the display case covers and placed it on the floor. Then, he waited, being sure to keep moving, triggering the motion sensors. As he put the painting down he looked at his watch and smiled, pleased with himself for being a little bit ahead of schedule.

After a few minutes two men dressed in blue police windbreakers came barging through the back door with guns raised. Louie put his hands in the air immediately as one of the men directed him to drop to his knees. The other man turned on the lights. The first man roughly pushed Louie to the ground, yanking his hands behind his back and putting on the tie wrap handcuffs. At that point Johnny walked in, surmised the situation, and spoke quickly to the second man. He then walked quickly into the exhibit area to assess for any damage. After a quick scan he walked back to the two men with the handcuffed man now standing, seemed to thank them, and then said something sternly to the handcuffed man who shot back an angry response.

As the two men in police jackets led the 'thief' out of the gallery, and the view of the cameras, Johnny was already dialing his phone.

"Hello?" Nina answered groggily.

"Nina, it's Johnny. There's been a break in at the gallery, but we got him."

"W-what?" Nina asked, obviously trying to process while waking up.

"A guy picked the lock of the back door and broke in. Looked like he was targeting a painting and one of the glass bowls, but the system picked it up and contacted me just like it was designed. The cops just took him away. There was no damage to any of the art."

"Um, wow, well that's good," Nina responded, "did you call Meya?"

"No, you were my first call. Honestly, I knew that you had some reservations about using us, so I guess I selfishly wanted to call you first. Sorry about that. Either way, the system worked. You wanted me to call Meya first?" he asked.

"No, no, that's fine," she replied, "I'll call her now."

"It will all be captured by the cameras so you two can come down and watch if you want."

"Oh, ok…thanks Johnny, I'm glad that we went with you. We'll be right down."

Later, back at the delicatessen, Louie tore into the two guys that portrayed the cops. "What the hell you two? Did you have to slam me down like that? You idiots think you're real cops, Christ!"

"Sorry Streets, had to make it look real," one of the men, Frankie "The Chin" Marconi, a fellow member of Sonny's crew, said while looking over and smiling at Nicky, the other fake cop.

"Real cute! You two are gonna get yours, mark my words!" Louie replied. Louie was furious, looking like he was getting ready for his own assault on the two men. "That shit hurt, about broke my shoulder," he said as he rotated his arm, "your turn will come, don't you two worry."

"Shut up, all of you", Sonny commanded entering the room. "You pulled it off again, Jewels. Saved your ass again too, Jakey, but no more screw ups, capiche?" A brief thought of his mother shot quickly through Jake's mind when he heard Sonny refer to him as 'Jakey', but he quickly pushed past it to focus on Sonny's warning. Everyone nodded with understanding of Sonny's direction. "Now, let's have a few drinks and get on with it," Sonny directed, evidently satisfied that the situation had been managed.

As the drinks started to be poured, Jake approached Sonny. Johnny was now sitting with him at a table. "So, does this make us square?" Jake asked, "I thought that was the deal."

Sonny studied him for a beat. Johnny said nothing. "That was the deal," Sonny replied. Jake felt some relief, but not as much as he had expected. Something still felt wrong. He knew that even if he was allowed to walk he would probably always be looking over his shoulder.

"But deals change," Sonny continued. "You got skills, kid. You're still of use to me. Ever handle a gun?" Sonny asked. Jake's face went ashen. Sonny continued, "If not, you're gonna. You're not done yet."

22

The day had finally come. Meya had been waiting with anticipation since she and Nina had set out on their venture. The art had arrived as promised and been installed as directed. They had held an open house. They had set up payment processing, security, and all of the other things to satisfy Meya's father, Jiao. Jiao had even added a few additional pieces from the family's collection. And now it was time for what Meya had been waiting for, for what she had been working towards, to get the praise that she longed for. It was time to show the gallery off to Dr. Chad Longfellow.

Nina was less enthused about the big unveil.

Chad had actually been instrumental in setting up the gallery by obtaining the majority of the pieces. He had used some creativity in quietly borrowing several pieces from the College's collection. The pieces had been loaned by the artists to the College for the annual show. Chad had conveniently moved the submission date a few months early to support this side venture. Chad had also included a few of his own paintings to be showcased. These pieces would be for sale along with only a select few others.

Meya stood in the main gallery, at times bouncing up and down slightly in anticipation, awaiting Chad's arrival. Nina worked in the office. Nina understood the importance of his efforts in helping to make the gallery a reality, but had barely been able to endure Meya's crush on the man for the past few years.

She shuddered slightly as she recalled some of Meya's running commentary on the 'journey of their relationship', as

Meya called it. Their relationship barometer ranged from "Chad and I have such a connection, it is almost surreal" to "he doesn't realize what he has in me" and back again to "we are truly just perfect together." Meya wrote him personal letters, bought him presents on anniversaries, and ran to him at his beck and call. Chad would fit her in when convenient, and was very skilled at realizing when he needed to feed her desires. An invite to a poetry reading, a late call to meet at his apartment, or the pinnacle, an invitation to an artist reception at the College were all it took to quickly relieve Meya's insecurities.

'That relationship is just a patronizing supply of ego leveraged at an insecure coed', Nina thought, *'of course I hitched my wagon to Meya for the same reasons, so who am I to criticize?'*

Chad let Meya know the previous week that he was 'coming to visit the gallery and her, the two things most on his mind.' Meya had been on cloud nine since she got his email. The gallery sparkled, the result of the excellent work of the cleaners for the neighboring office Meya had convinced to work second shift to ready the gallery for Chad's arrival. She wore a black dress that shimmered slightly as she moved with four inch heels and a single strand of pearls around her neck. Her hair was pulled back with a complimentary pearl ended hairpin just the way Chad likes it. She even managed to get an 8:00 pm reservation at Savourer, the hip new French restaurant.

As the large red door slid open, Dr. Chad Longfellow strode into the gallery with his usual air of arrogance. Walking as upright as possible to maximize the height of his average frame he gazed left and right with his eyes finally resting on Meya. "Chad! You're here," exclaimed Meya, moving quickly to greet him, with hands clasped in front of her, fingers intertwined nervously.

"Hello Meya," Chad replied simply, holding her shoulders and offering a quick kiss on her forehead. He then shifted his focus again back to the gallery and its offerings.

Meya had told him all about the gallery, and even sent a few pictures, but he still chose to soak it all in on his own. He moved slowly along first the outer wall taking in the displays. He turned to meticulously take in the pieces on pedestals and along the inner wall. "You were right about these West facing windows and the contribution of the natural light," he commented after covering over half of the gallery. Despite the compliment, he still noted a few subtle lighting adjustments that he wanted to have made. After a few more minutes of observation and study he paused at a pedestal with a statue of a woman in bronze staring at such an angle that made it difficult for the viewer to match her line of sight. The piece was one that was on loan, and a favorite of Chads. "Perhaps pondering a past event or maybe a future tribulation." Meya smiled with adoration at Chad's insightful thought.

In general, he was pleased to see the paintings arranged in the manner that he had prescribed, interspersing some of the abstract works with some of the more classical themes. He was not pleased, however, with the placement of his own paintings. His paintings had been moved from his desired location near the entrance to the gallery, where customers could take in the pieces, consider as they made their way through the rest of the gallery, and then end near the office area where conversation with Meya or Nina might occur to finalize a sale. Instead, there were three complimentary Asian scroll paintings. The scroll paintings were accented with a jade sculpture under glass on a pedestal in front of them.

"Why are my pieces not where I want them to be?" Chad asked.

"Well," Meya began to reply sheepishly, "my father provided these pieces from our family collection and he thought they might add another dimension to the gallery."

Chad stepped back and studied the pieces. The three scroll paintings hung vertically, with each panel providing an individual scene that told a story when hung together. The leftmost panel depicted an Asian style home nestled in front of a mountain with the land winding around a body of water to the bottom of the panel. The rightmost panel depicted a fishing boat tied to a pier with a winding path also ending at the bottom of the panel. The center panel depicted a fisherman with a long pole over his shoulder walking on the path that connects all three panels. The center panel also provided a mountain peak in the background and birds flying in the sky. The pieces contained no colors, but had intricate shading within the black and white palette that brought depth to all three pieces.

He then shifted his focus to the figure under glass on the pedestal. The figure appeared to be carved stone. The majority of the stone held a subtle green hue, with a few areas of a mottled yellowish brown. The figure was striking with a head similar to a lion, but with horns. The figure also had four wings with four powerful legs crouched as if ready to attack. The head and front shoulders of the piece were also turned and tilted slightly to further convey a sense of coiled motion, as if the mythical beast were on the precipice of striking.

Not wanting to admit that he had no real knowledge of Asian art, Chad asked Meya to tell him about the pieces. "Meya, these are fascinating specimens. Please tell me about them from you and your family's perspective."

Still hesitant that Chad would disapprove, Meya began to explain, "Well, these have been in our family for generations. The scroll paintings depict life in my great-great-grandfather's village many years ago. My father included them to remind me that our family has built all that we have from a humble fishing beginning. He felt the reminder would be encouraging to me as Nina and I try to make this gallery work." She waited for Chad to respond, but he didn't at first, holding his gaze on the paintings.

Finally, he returned his attention to her, "And the statuette?"

"That is a bixie," Meya replied.

"What is a bixie?" Chad asked, genuinely curious about the new term.

"A bixie is a traditional mythological creature believed to be able to ward off evil forces with its magical powers. This one is carved out of jade, but has stained some over the years. I think that makes it look better, personally. You can probably figure out why my father included that as well."

"You know, Meya, normally I would have replied that while your father is an expert in business, he is not an expert in art like me. However," Chad continued while shifting positions to fully take in the bixie figure, "I have to agree with him on this one. Your father, and you, have a wonderful eye," he finished, shifting to look at Meya, and offering her his best smile.

Moving toward her, he held her hands in his, then lifted her chin to look at him. "And we need to have things just so, right my dear?" Nina, who had been listening from the back room, rolled her eyes at this comment. "Now, my dear Meya, what shall we do this evening?" Chad asked.

"I have a surprise for you tonight. Savourer at 8:00," she said to him looking for his approval.

Chad replied smoothly, "Wonderful, I can't wait, and then maybe you can show me the city on the way back to my hotel?"

Meya smiled back proudly, and the two turned to leave. "Bye Nina, we'll finish up tomorrow."

'*Sure we will*', thought Nina as she waved goodbye, relieved to see Chad leave.

23

"I think we just gotta do it." Sonny said to no one in particular, thinking out loud. "Yeah, that's the only play here."

Sonny, Johnny, Nicky, and Louie were the only four remaining in the delicatessen back room. Sonny was sitting at one table, Johnny and Louie at another. Nicky was at the small corner bar mixing drinks for he and the other men. Sonny had sent Jake away with a stern warning, "loose lips sink ships, if you get me." Jake had barely heard it in his haze of realization that his time with the Mafia was not at an end. He nodded absently.

"You walk him out," Sonny instructed Frankie, the other fake cop.

"C'mon kid, you heard him." Jake rose and made his way out the back door and into the night.

"So," Sonny started again as soon as the door clicked shut, "I figure we keep the job small, just the four of us."

Johnny knew what Sonny was thinking, but had to ask anyway. "Sonny, you thinking of knocking over the gallery? You heard what Arch said."

"I know what Arch said," Sonny replied in a surprisingly calm manner. Johnny had expected an explosion of backlash typical of what he had experienced in the past. "At some point we gotta make a move to make this thing bigger than it is, either for the family or for ourselves." Louie nodded his agreement. Nicky went back to making drinks.

Sonny could sense the apprehension from some of the men. "I know that you all think this is a lack of loyalty to the family, but it's not. This will bring the family back into the fold, make us major players again. All of us." He paused taking a second to stare at each man, partially to emphasize his point and partially to get a read of their reactions. "We do this right, and no one will get hurt. Plus, we will have stayed on our turf, and Silvio and Archie can take all of the credit and get a nice cut." Sonny looked at Nicky, and then at Louie who was again nodding slightly at the opportunity. "Look, I get it," Sonny continued, "but I'm telling you I won't say a word and neither will any of you. All of the credit goes up on this one. Plus, no drugs or other stuff that Silvio and The Commission hate. Best for the family and best for business. That is why we need to keep this small. Only the three that I can trust the most...you three."

This was a clear departure from how Sonny usually operated. At times a loose cannon, he never talked about, or let alone ever displayed, a willingness not to be in the spotlight taking credit wherever he could. He also held fast to the Mafia credo that respect was paid up when it came to a crew, and that when he gave the orders, the orders were to be followed. No exceptions. There was something different this time, like he actually had thought through the big picture, and was asking rather than directing. Johnny thought, '*Man, I've never seen him like this, he must really want the guys to buy in.*'

Sonny knew that he just needed a little of the right incentive to really get their agreement. He planned to break through any final barriers with the one thing that resonated most with these guys...money. "I understand that Archie said 'No'," Sonny continued, readying to play his trump card, "but here's what I'll do...equal cut for each of you. You don't even have to kick up, I'll cover it." This was unheard of.

Made guys always got a cut, and paid a cut of that up to the next level. "You hear me guys, that is how important I think this is for the family."

Sonny could see that this was starting to resonate with at least Louie and now Nicky, but continued pushing. "Nicky, you can always use more for your mother," Sonny continued, knowing that Nicky's mother was elderly and relied on Nicky to help make ends meet. "Johnny, I know that you know how to make a few more C-notes work," a veiled reference to Johnny's love of gambling without calling him out on it. "And Streets, I'm sure you can use the extra scratch to take care of that issue you got on the side, right? Another mouth to feed ain't free." Sonny was referring to the woman that accused Louie of 'knocking her up', and was now looking for child support.

Both Nicky and Johnny immediately turned to look at Louie with surprised looks. They didn't know this. Louie had come to Sonny for advice on the matter privately. "Yeah," was Louie's simple reply to the revelation, his features held steady but his face flush with anger at the betrayal.

"Ok, so are we all in on this thing or what?" Sonny asked. The three men looked around the room at each other, trying to confirm that each man had been sold on the benefit to the family, or at least using it as an excuse to justify the move and the extra money. They all returned their gaze to Sonny, each nodding agreement and commitment to the job.

"Good," Sonny said, with a mix of satisfaction and relief. He raised his glass to the other men who raised theirs in response. "Alla famiglia!" Sonny toasted, meaning 'to the family'. After each man took a drink, Sonny continued, "So I've been thinking this through, and I got a plan. First, we need to get into the building. Figure we'll just do what we did last time and unlock the window during the day like we did for Street's fake robbery. That worked last time."

"Then I figure we pose as cleaners, make our way in after everyone is gone, go up to the gallery, disable the alarm, lift the stuff, and carry it out making it look like cleaning stuff. We can use the van again." The three men nodded at the plan, but waited silently for Johnny's adjustments, as he had done so many times before.

"Yeah, Sonny, I gotcha," Johnny said as he always did, trying to ease into his comments. He sat back in his chair, purposely keeping his actions very passive. "I do have a couple of things, though."

"Sure, whadda ya got, Jewels?" was Sonny's surprising response, again out of character from his usual brash behavior.

"Uh, yeah, so I'm thinking maybe being cleaners ain't the best option. We need a better way to conceal moving the stuff. How about we be movers instead of cleaners?" Johnny continued, "We can use some big boxes on those furniture mover things with the wheels."

"That's better," Louie, evidently still worked up, interjected. Sonny turned to Louie and shot him a quick look. He was dying to shoot a putdown his way, but resisted not wanting to tip the delicate balance he had established.

"Anyway," continued Johnny, "there is also a security company that comes and makes rounds inside the building a few times a night. There are two of them that seem to trade off different nights. We need to avoid that."

"Nicky, you scout the place and figure out our time window to do the job," Sonny directed.

"How long we gonna need?" Nicky asked.

"I figure an hour or two to be safe. Should be less, but that gives us time if anything comes up," Johnny replied.

"We'll all be heavy too," Sonny said, referring to each of them carrying a gun.

"We'll need tools to take the paintings down, and blankets to wrap the glass pieces," Louie added, now focusing more on the job. "It will be faster than pulling them from the frames and better than cutting them out."

"I'll visit next week and try to figure out what things we should target. Higher value stuff. Too bad we can't talk to Archie's fence to find out what he thinks he can move," Johnny added, realizing instantly that this had been a mistake.

"I cannot be clear enough on this…no one says anything to anyone, especially Archie…youz got it?" Sonny said slowly in a low threatening voice. "I asked if youz got it?" he asked again, his temper starting to rise.

"I got it Sonny…we got it. No one's saying anything, Boss," Johnny replied, thankful that the instant rage was slowly released from Sonny's features.

"Anything else?" Sonny asked again, sitting back and finishing his drink. Nicky started to make him another.

"Finally, when we turn off the security system with the code, the system continues to record. A feature of the system that Nina wanted after our fake robbery. So, do you know how to disable the cameras?" Sonny asked Johnny.

"No," he replied, "but I know who does." Everyone in the room knew that he was referring to Jake.

Sonny chuckled quietly to himself, saying "I knew that kid would be useful again."

"Yeah, he can drive the van too, act as a lookout and make it easier to get out of there quickly," Johnny added.

"Perfect, we'll promise him that this will be his last job," Sonny said laughing to himself again, "dumb kid is never going to be done with us."

"That it?" Sonny asked.

"Yeah, actually, I think that is it, other than we have to find a fence on the downlow," Johnny replied.

"Yeah, I'll figure that out," Sonny replied, "I have a few contacts around." Johnny held his poker face in front of Sonny, masking his frustration that Sonny's 'contacts' either weren't very helpful or were non-existent.

"I got a guy too," Louie quickly added. "I've used him before, he's good. I can take care of it if you want."

Sonny looked at Louie skeptically, but was pretty much stuck agreeing to it to keep the momentum going with his crew. "Ok then, we'll use your guy, Streets. Sounds like we have a plan. Nicky, you tell me as soon as you get a bead on the two security guys so that we can pick a time. I want to do this soon, so stay on it."

"Got it Sonny," Nicky replied with a single nod.

"O.K...to the plan and the rise of the Amoretti family," Sonny again raised his glass in a toast, with the others following suit.

To the plan', Louie thought, still resenting Sonny's reveal of his secret. *'To my plan, Sonny, to my plan.'*

24

"I friggin' knew it," Archie said, shaking his head and looking at Dominic.

Dominic swirled his vino in the small glass, taking drinks between drags on his fat cigar. He replied in his baritone voice thick with an Italian accent, "Yeah, you saw it comin'...che cavolo."

"Yeah, really not good," Archie replied, interpreting Dominic's Italian and nodding slightly.

"Streets, you did the right thing by telling me," Archie said, now turning to look at Louie who was the only other person in the room. Louie was tired of being treated like a second-class citizen on the crew and still angry at Nicky and Frankie also had roughed him up unnecessarily after the staged robbery. He had done as much to make Sonny money as anyone else, except maybe Johnny who was the one person that didn't abuse him. Sonny's treatment, however, was consistent and degrading. Never one to swallow abuse for long, things had reached a boiling point with Louie, even if he needed the opportunity the family provided him.

Louie was now standing in front of the family's consigliere and underboss. While happy to be sticking it to Sonny and the others in his crew, he also knew that he was taking a big risk by going over Sonny's head to Archie and Dominic. Archie's initial response had calmed his fear only slightly, knowing that behaviors could turn on a moment's notice in these situations especially if Sonny found out that he had made this move.

"Does that jamoke actually think that I wouldn't hear about this?" Archie asked.

"I dunno. I think he thinks you and the Boss will be happy with him once he pulls it off," Dominic replied.

"Yeah, and good for his reputation if it doesn't bring us too much heat. Not to mention he may end up gutting his grandfather again if the whole thing turns south," Archie responded. "I told them that there's heat on this kind of thing now, after O'Connel and his crew got pinched for the same damn thing."

"Alright Streets, why don't you go take a walk," Archie directed. Louie knew that this meant he was to go away and come back later so that Archie and Dominic could talk. At this he nodded, turned, and left.

Archie slammed his fist down on the table. "You know Dom, I'm getting real tired of this kid," he said in a menacing tone.

"Fugget about it," Dom replied in deep baritone agreement.

"Now I gotta figure out if we take it up or not. We been down this road before. Gonna cost time and resources again, plus the old man," Archie considered, talking with his hands in sharp movements, sighing as he finished speaking.

"Plus we got Streets jumping Sonny, showing no respect," Dominic added, referring to one of the most sacred pillars of the Mafia...respect. Respect of the family, respect of the hierarchy, and respect of the business. Both Archie and Dominic, as old timers, lived and died by this credo and knew the repercussions when it wasn't followed. "I mean when we were coming up you never went against a made guy, and if you did that was it."

"Yeah, Costa Nostra, 'Our Thing', meant something then. Doesn't seem to mean anything with the new guys," Archie replied in agreement. "Plus, if his guys are willing to turn like this, maybe Sonny isn't managing his crew as he should. That could be dangerous."

"Sonny has always been wild…," Dominic added.

"…and looking to make his reputation with the Commission," Archie said, finishing Dominics thought. "What's also bugging me is that I don't know what's causing Louie to turn on Sonny like that. I mean Sonny can be a real prick to those guys, but I ain't never seen it to the level of doing this," Archie further considered out loud.

"More new school behavior, maybe," Dominic responded.

"Yeah, but if that behavior comes that easy now, then what happens if they get picked up. How long before they talk then?" Archie asked with concern, referring to talking to the authorities if they got arrested.

Maybe we need to handle it differently this time," Dom offered, staring down at his wine.

"What are you thinking?" Archie asked, pretty sure that he knew where the old-timer was heading.

"This crew does alright earning, but it always comes with a price. And if word gets out that they directly defied you and you did nothing about it…well, you know."

"Yeah, I know. Loss of face, loss of respect, loss of territory…all of it."

The two men sat silently for a moment, as Dominic took a drink of his wine and Archie stared down at the floor.

Leaning in after a bit, Archie finally asked Dominic, "You really want to go there?"

Dominic took a long drag of his cigar, then blew the thick, white smoke into the air. "I've been giving this some thought.

The kid is a constant problem, for us and the old man. He's careless, which is dangerous. The other crews are earning well and can easily take Sonny's rackets." Dominic continued, "Plus, we need to set an example. We don't want the other families to see us as weak, which will happen if Sonny disobeying you gets out."

"I think we gotta take 'em out."

This statement hung in the air as both men contemplated. Archie rubbed his chin. Dominic stayed in the same position, staring at the drink he was swirling in his hand.

"Yeah, I suppose we do," Archie finally stated. "It will kill the old man though, and he will never authorize the hit."

"I know, but he has blinders to Sonny," Dominic said, sitting up in his chair and leaning closer to Archie. "Arch, you and I both know that back in the day this would have been handled long before now."

"I know," Archie said, now looking directly at Dominic, "but Dom, it's gonna kill him."

"Maybe, but it's better his heartbreak than any of us, including the old man, losing this thing of ours."

"Actually, I'm thinking maybe we don't tell Sil," Archie postulated.

Archie went back to staring at the floor in contemplation. Both men sat silently for a few seconds, letting this statement hang in the air. Archie then continued, "That would really be pushing the limits of our credo, but we'd be doing it for the family. No personal advantage for us, probably makes our situation harder in the near term." Archie paused again, and then continued, "But it would be better for the long term position of the family."

"Gonna take a tight crew," Dominic said, understanding that Archie wanted to do the hit outside of normal channels.

"Gonna need someone that won't talk...ever," he added. "Yeah, maybe I can get my cousins from Providence to come down and help us out. They all don't like Sonny anyways too, if we even need them," Dominic added, "I mean we got the element of surprise and all, and Sonny's crew will be focused on robbing the place."

Archie nodded, but had already moved on to the new challenge of keeping everything from Silvio. "I think I may have an idea of how to keep this from Sil. Shit, Louie just gave it to me."

"What's that?" Dominic asked.

"We pose as cops just like they did with that fake robbery to cover the security system install. Make our way in after them and surprise them. We call the actual cops once things are over, take off, and it all looks like the robbery ended in a shootout. We can actually use the cop jackets that Johnny had Nicky and Frankie use for the fake robbery when that kid they used to install the system thought he was made," Archie explained.

"That might actually work," Dominic replied, now sitting back and thinking things through. "Even so, even though it worked for them, still a lot of risk. We need to know their plan to make our side foolproof."

"Yeah," Archie said contemplating. "Go get Streets, will you? He should be back from his walk by now. I got an idea."

Dominic walked into the front of the delicatessen. Louie had returned and was sitting at a table drinking a San Pellegrino. A simple nod of Dominic's head told Louie that the two were now ready for him to return to the back room. As they entered, Dominic again took his seat while Louie stood before them.

"Streets, me and Dom have been talking. After further consideration we are actually in agreement with Sonny." Louie's eyebrows raised and he nearly dropped his soda. Dominic was surprised by the statement as well, but let his experience take over and held his poker face. "It would be a good move for the family. Low risk with the security system in our control, and we're sure that Johnny did his usual expert job casing the place."

"Now don't worry, coming to us was the right thing," Archie continued, "we want to keep this from Silvio as well. He will never endorse it as you know, but would benefit from it all the same." Archie didn't add that Silvio also wouldn't endorse it because he didn't want to risk losing his grandson. That thought only lived between he and Dominic.

"We aren't going to endorse it to Sonny because we don't want it getting back to Silvio if things go wrong. Sonny wants to take on this risk with his crew, that is his decision to make. We are endorsing it to you, so you can be assured we won't do anything to interfere, especially since you came forward respectfully."

Louie was still trying to process this unexpected turn of events when Archie asked him to fill them in on the plan. Louie had jeopardized a lot by coming to the two men, allowing his temper and pride to control his actions. He was committed now, though, and so he began to run through the plan. He covered the fact that they were going to keep it just to their crew and were going to disguise themselves as movers, and also included that Jake would be part of the crew to give them access to the building and the gallery.

"How you gonna fence the stuff?" Dominic asked as Louie finished talking.

"I have a guy from way back. I can get him and make an introduction if you want," Louie replied.

"No, not necessary. You're a standup guy," Archie responded, further surprising, and pleasing Louie.

"Ok, we got it." Archie was wrapping up the meeting. "Let us know when it's gonna happen and if anything changes. We want this to go. Oh, and Streets, if anyone finds out about this, as far as they will know a little birdie told us about this. Don't worry though, Dom and I won't forget who."

Louie's brow furrowed. While he was still unnerved by the men's unexpected positive reaction to the job, it was Archie's final statement that most bothered Louie. *'Dom and I won't forget who...not sure what that means'*, he thought. It really didn't matter though, the move was made and whatever fallout was coming was going to happen.

'Sonny, Nicky, and Frankie will definitely get it worse than me if things go bad', Louie hoped.

25

Jake hoped that returning to the restaurant would calm himself down some. Seeing Sarah would calm him even more, he hoped. He had just left the back room of the delicatessen, and was making his way across the street to The Athena. Rain spit from the sky, and the gusty wind whipped around the corner as if pushing him away from the entrance to the restaurant. After an especially strong gust rocked him back on his heels he stepped again towards the restaurant entrance, opening the door and stepping inside.

Sarah greeted him immediately with a tight embrace once she realized it was Jake. "Is it over?" she asked with hope in her eyes. She was wearing her standard waitress outfit, but was clearly less put together than usual. Before Jake could answer, the door to the restaurant opened again, allowing a gust of wind to sweep into the space. In the doorway stood Louie. Both Jake and Sarah's eyes widened at the appearance of the gangster.

Louie made his way to Jake and Sarah. "We need to talk," he said to Jake. Jake and Sarah were now clutching each other's hand. "But maybe not in here," Louie added, turning to look at Sarah, then back at Jake, "c'mon." Jake followed Louie outside and around the corner to block the wind and get some privacy. "So here's the deal. You meet us at the back room at 5:00 when we go. Not sure when yet, so keep this on at all times." Louie handed Jake a burner cell phone. "I'll call you when it is a go. It will likely be in the next few days. You'll be driving the van and disabling the security system.

Should be pretty easy for you. You got it?" Louie explained. Jake just nodded.

"No good, kid, I need to hear you say it. You got it or what?" Louie responded.

"Yeah, I got it," Jaked mumbled despondently.

"Kid, it'll be fine. It's all set up. Easy in and easy out." With this, Louie gave Jake a single nod, turned, and said as he walked away, "Just be ready".

Jake stood on the sidewalk letting the news continue to sink in. After a minute, he turned and walked back to the restaurant, again fighting his way through the strong wind. Jake didn't have to say anything more for Sarah to understand. Her face briefly dropped in reaction to Jake still being pulled into work for the Mafia, but she regained her composure quickly. "C'mon, let's head to the back and you can fill me in. Pedro can cover the front. It's light anyway."

They again stood in the kitchen in nearly in the same spots where their romance had first taken root, except this time the mood was far from the exciting, magnetic mood they shared the first time they cooked together.

Sarah knew Jake had installed the security system as his act of penance for attacking the mobsters. She did not know about the fake robbery. Jake decided to fill her in on all of it. "I was concerned that one of the women at the gallery had recognized me from when we went to the open house," he started.

"Do you mean the woman, Nina?" Sarah asked.

"Yeah, I think that's it, the one we talked to. Anyway, I told Johnny, he seems to be the guy in charge of handling the gallery, and they staged a fake robbery of the place!"

Sarah's eyes widened at this comment. "They staged a robbery. That place must really be worth something to them."

"Yeah, I agree. They pulled it off though, and the women at the gallery are more convinced than ever that the system is legit."

"So you're done then," Sarah said matter-of-factly, "you did what they asked."

"I thought so too, but no. The head Mob guy, Sonny, said that deals change, and I'm not done yet. And now Louie tells me that I'm part of a robbery."

Sarah's eyes widened even more when she heard this. She instinctively crossed her arms and looked away from Jake. Jake moved forward and put his hands on her shoulders, turning her to look at him again.

"I didn't tell you because I wasn't positive that anything would come of it, and didn't say anything more at the time." Sarah lowered her folded arms slightly, but not entirely.

At this Sarah moved away from Jake. She walked across the room and stood facing away from him. After a moment of silence she asked without turning, "So, are you going to do it?"

Jake walked towards her, responding, "I have to, what choice do I have?"

"You could leave. We could leave...together," Sarah said, turning to Jake and looking deep into his eyes with the same look of hope she had when he entered the restaurant. Feeling her emotion through her gaze, Jake felt the old feelings of fear and the strong desire to leave again. This time with Sarah.

"No! You cannot leave," an irate Zehab exclaimed as he burst into the kitchen. He had obviously been listening from the storeroom. "How can you continue to be so stupid? They will just find you, haven't you yet figured out that these guys are dangerous and mean business?"

"Have you been listening to us the entire time?" Jake asked angrily.

"Yes, and is a good thing I was. You run and they will find you," Zehab replied. His concern was focused more on his business than Jake or Sarah. He didn't want to risk losing his restaurant to the mobsters. "These guys don't forget being disrespected. Also, you know the plan or at least some of it, enough of it. You are a loose end. The Mafia ties up loose ends."

Jake felt the walls of the kitchen closing in. He and Sarah being together depended on his decision. The fate of the restaurant depended on his decision. And most importantly his and likely Sarah's lives depended on his decision. He came to the city to get away from hardship and pain, and now the demon had found him again.

Jake suddenly had a strong desire to clear his head and think in the best way he knew how. "I gotta go," he declared heading for the door.

Sarah, grabbing her coat in the front room, followed him out the door, calling after Jake, "Wait I'm coming too."

Sarah caught up to Jake just as he fired up the Yamaha. The rain had stopped, but a breeze was still blowing. She stood in front of the motorcycle, as if in a standoff with it. Jake knew that he wasn't going to be able to ride off without her, and deep down he didn't want to. He unclipped the extra helmet that Red had given him *'in case he ever managed to actually land a girl'* and handed it to Sarah. She climbed on behind Jake and wrapped her arms around him. They then sped off into the night.

After a few hours they had cleared the city congestion and made their way to the hills of the country near the Delaware Water Gap. They turned off the highway, and proceeded to wind through the secondary roads. Pacing along the Delaware River they both appreciated the cool country air, tracking the moonlight as it danced out from behind the clouds reflecting on the water as they rode along.

Jake used the time to consider his options, not that he had many. When his mind tired of trying to solve his problem with the Mafia, it drifted to other thoughts. He loved feeling Sarah on his back, her arms wrapped tightly around his waist. Her warmth and embrace were new feelings for him on the machine. He felt so lucky to find her, and was really starting to care for her. He was pretty sure that she was falling for him as well.

He also thought about his mother and Red. How he had left them both in their time of need, unable to deal with his own emotions, let alone theirs. He felt pretty confident that neither would be mad at him for leaving, but also that each would rather he be in Pine Grove. *'Well, maybe not Red'*, he thought, *'he always preached that I should be my own man. He also preached that I should find a girl.'*

This last thought brought a small but short-lived smile to Jake's face. His success at the restaurant also drifted into his mind on the tail of the other thoughts, both his newfound cooking talent as well as finding Sarah. Even his ability to cross the Mafia and still be alive seemed in some ways a twisted success. *'Maybe the move to the city hasn't been a total failure after all'*, he thought, *'all I have to do now is just figure out how to get away from the Mob. C'mon, Jake, think...for her.'*

After a bit they stopped in a parking area along a large reservoir to stretch their legs and talk. "I'm still not sure what to do, Sarah," he confessed, the stress evident in his features.

"I know, I have been trying to think it through as well the entire ride out here," Sarah replied. "Jake, I just want to be with you," Sarah continued, "I have never met someone who cares for me like you do. I've never met anyone who has your abilities either that would be even remotely interested in someone like me."

Jake looked at Sarah, confused. "What abilities? The ability to put both of our lives in jeopardy?"

"I know, but put that aside for a second. You came into that restaurant out of nowhere and learned to cook those dishes almost overnight. You repair all kinds of things, and even installed that security system. And honestly, the way you protected the restaurant and me, while mis-directed, was amazingly honorable. I have never met anyone like you. Jake, like I said, I want to be with you. I don't care if we run. I have been running for years. I know that I'll feel safe with you. Let's just keep riding and never look back." Tears began to well in Sarah's eyes.

Jake felt a glimmer of pride ignite inside his chest as he processed Sarah's words, now beginning to resonate with some of his earlier thoughts. He had never really thought of his actions in a positive light, always considering them passive and cowardly efforts to keep loss at bay and allay his fears. But she had seen the opposite in him, just as Red had. Maybe it was time for him to see things that way, too.

He felt closer to this woman than he had to anyone else in a long time, even Red. He knew that he was falling in love. "No Sarah, I am done running," he responded resolutely, wrapping his arms around her, holding her. Sarah laid her head on Jake's chest. She had her own demons from her past, and sought the same sense of security as, and now in, Jake.

The couple stood embraced in the moonlight in silence, savoring the solace they found in each other. Sarah broke the silence first. "Jake, I'm with you," she said looking into his eyes, "in whatever you want to do, but we do it together."

"Sarah, I need to be the man I want to be, and he isn't someone who always runs. I need to be strong and finish this. We can't always be looking over our shoulder. I'll do this last job, and then we'll both walk away, together. I will have done enough to have paid my debt. We'll have to leave the rest to fate."

"Fate seems awfully risky, Jake, for both you and me...for us."

"Actually, I have an idea on how to help our chances." Jake pulled the burner phone that the Mafia had given him. "They gave me this to call me when it's time for the job. The thing is, it takes pictures too."

"Wait, you're not thinking of...," Sarah replied with a look of concern growing on her face.

"It may be our only real way out. I take some pictures of the robbery and I have some leverage. They never have to know about it, but we can use them," Jake said.

"They will kill you if you try to blackmail them. You can't take it to them, Jake, it's too dangerous," Sarah cautioned worriedly.

"Maybe I won't take it to them. Maybe I'll take it to the Feds."

Sarah considered this with a long pause. "So, witness protection?"

"Yeah, if it comes to that," Jake replied.

"Ok," Sarah replied softly, trying her best to smile at Jake, "a change of identity might not be such a bad thing as long as we're together." He kissed her deeply, and held her one more time.

Finally, he said while looking up at the sky, "We'd better head back, I feel a storm coming."

26

"In at 7:00 out by 10:00, right?" Sonny asked.

"Yeah, the daytime guard walks the building between 4:00 and 5:00 p.m. then leaves with most everyone else. Another guard doesn't show up until around midnight, walks the place, and leaves by 2:00 a.m. They must do multiple places. The daytime guard shows up again at 7:30 in the morning for the day," Nicky confirmed. "The building is always empty by 7:00 at night, and it just looks like we are working to stay outta there during the day".

"Alright, get it together then, almost time to leave."

The irony of Sonny's words hung over Jake. He had uttered these same words when it was time to run from Pine Grove. He had heard Sarah use these same words when it was time for her to leave West Virginia behind. Sarah had also tried to convince Jake that maybe it was time for both of them to leave to stop Jake from carrying through on the robbery. But Jake had decided that these words no longer framed a sense of escape, but rather, fear and immaturity. He was done running. He had to finish things with the Mob so that he and Sarah could move forward without always looking over their shoulders. One more job.

"I do this and I'm done, right?" Jake asked when Sonny and Johnny again walked him through the job.

"Yeah, you do this and we're square," Sonny replied. Jake knew that was the best that he would get from the gangster. He also knew that it was likely not the truth, and that they would ultimately call on him as much as they wanted. But he would have leverage with the photos taken on the burner phone if things went right.

They had obtained moving coveralls, dollies, and large cardboard boxes from another friend of the Family. For Jake, his part was simple. Drive them over in the van, go in and disconnect the alarm system, and then head back to the van and wait. However, things quickly got more complicated when Johnny approached him. "You know how to use one of these?" Johnny asked, handing him a small, black Smith & Wesson revolver.

Jake picked it up knowingly. The black .38 special had a worn wooden grip and scratched serial number. The gun was loaded, which Jake confirmed by rotating the cylinder out of the gun as Red had taught him. "Yeah, I've used a pistol before to shoot at targets," Jake replied. He was comfortable with the firearm, but not the proposition of shooting someone, even with his newfound resolve to finish this one last job.

"You shouldn't need to use this, but just in case all hell breaks loose you need something." Jake didn't feel any safer with it.

They all loaded into the van, and Jake drove them over to the gallery at 7:00 sharp. When they arrived, Louie climbed the same fire escape to the same window that had again been left unlocked by Johnny's girlfriend. Instead of heading straight to the gallery like last time, Louie made his way downstairs and opened the door to the back entrance. Jake quickly backed the van up close to the back entrance. The four mobsters then began to unload the van and stage equipment for the job. They constructed the large boxes, then mounted them to the specially designed dollies. They next loaded straps, a few necessary tools to remove the art pieces, and moving blankets into the boxes, finally covering each with a draped blanket just in case anyone was still in the building. Finally, Nicky grabbed the step ladder.

While this was happening, Jake had gone ahead to disable the gallery security system. He had been given a key to the gallery this time, no doubt stolen or copied by one of the others, and quickly entered the master code in the keypad by the door. The gallery space was softly illuminated by the city and streetlights, with shadows falling throughout. This gave the gallery an ominous feeling in Jake's mind, no doubt fueled by the impending crime and all that came with it. Jake found himself momentarily transfixed by one of the paintings. The shadowed effects across the textured surface of the paint masked the vibrance of the image everywhere except for the bright red circle meant to serve as the foundation for the piece. Jake hoped that he and Sarah would be the red circle, burning their way through the shadows of his time in the city and finding their way free.

"Kid, we good?" Sonny barked from the door, breaking Jake's concentration.

"Yeah," Jake shouted back, snapping from his trance, "all clear."

"Good, now head back down to the van and wait for us to come out."

Jake had set up in the driver's seat of the van, the pistol laying beside him on the passenger seat at the ready but hidden under an extra moving blanket in case someone surprised him. He had decided that he would wait a few minutes before sneaking back in to take pictures of the crime. While there wasn't any real activity in the alley, he could see passersby still moving about on the sidewalk, and vehicles passing on the street. All were oblivious to the crime going on above them. He wondered how often he had passed by a crime and never even knew.

Suddenly a black SUV pulled into the alley and parked a few feet from the gallery back entrance, surprising Jake. He quickly slumped down in his seat to hide himself, and his hand subconsciously reached towards the gun. Jake quickly caught himself, pulling his hand away. *'Keep it together, Jake, it's just another vehicle. Could be anything'*, he thought to himself. After a minute, two men stepped out of the SUV. Both were in blue jackets as best he could see. As he watched, one of the men pulled a gun from his waistband, and then worked the slide to load a bullet into the chamber. Jake froze, instant panic surging through him. With eyes wide, Jake tried to process the scene unfolding in front of him.

The passenger then walked around the back of the SUV to talk to the driver. Jake could see 'POLICE' in bold white block letters on the back of his jacket. Jake was stunned. He recognized those jackets. They were legit, just like those the gangsters had worn for the fake robbery. Jake was completely unsure what to do, not knowing if he should try to warn the others or drive off saving himself. As Jake panicked pondering his next action, the men started to walk towards him. Jake quickly slipped to the back of the van and covered himself with one of the moving blankets. A minute later he heard one of the men speak as he looked into the back of the van. "Looks like they're in there. Let's go," a voice with a deep Italian accent called out.

Jake couldn't believe it. They hadn't even entered the van. They hadn't called it in. This all didn't make any sense. Uncovering himself Jake tried to make sense of what was going on. *'There's no sign of the security service. There're no cameras back here. The van is unmarked. I didn't tell anyone about this.* *Those guys wouldn't tell anyone about this except the guys that outrank them, and they wouldn't tell anyone about it.''*

He then realized that he had heard that voice before. Almost as suddenly as the panic had set in initially, a new revelation consumed him. *'Those weren't real cops, they were gangsters.'*

That's when Jake heard gunshots.

27

The shooting had stopped. What had sounded like a small war to Jake lasted only a few minutes. At first the terror and shock froze Jake in the back of the van. Snapping free of his initial shock, Jake immediately felt the urge to flee. *'I gotta get the hell outta here!'*, he thought to himself, climbing into the front seat to leave. As he made his way from the back of the van he looked down at the cell phone that had fallen onto the front seat. Jake paused, only briefly, but long enough to allow his mind to reach a new realization. *'No. I have to get the pictures…I have to get us out of this'*, he thought, thinking of himself and Sarah.

With as much resolve as he could muster, Jake crawled out of the van and stepped cautiously into the building.

It was silent at first as Jake made his way to the stairs. He opened the back stairwell door, paused, and listened. Still nothing. He quickly made his way up the stairs, pausing again at the door to the third floor. Jake opened the door only slightly. The silence was broken with Sonny's voice booming, along with crashing and movement. "I'm going after him!" Sonny yelled. Jake immediately saw a blur of someone run by, and then heard the door open to the fire escape. The piercing alarm screeched into the hallways, stopping when the door latched. Opening the stairwell door a little more, he saw Sonny running along the same path with a pistol drawn and what appeared to be blood on his face.

He wasn't sure if Sonny saw him, so he quickly closed the stairwell door. Again, he heard the piercing of the fire door alarm briefly, followed by banging footsteps and shouting from outside. As suddenly as the chase had started it stopped, and all that Jake could hear was his own rapid breaths echoing in the stairwell. After a few seconds, he again opened the door slightly. This time he heard nothing, he saw nothing.

Jake slowly made his way out of the stairwell and into the third floor lobby. The smell of gunfire filled the air. A lamp had been knocked over, the shade laying nearby in pieces. It was at that moment Jake realized that in all of the commotion he had forgotten to bring the gun. *'Brilliant, Jake'*, he thought, deciding that there was no turning back at this point. He hugged the wall of the lobby and made his way to the gallery back entrance. As he poked his head around the doorway entrance Jake could not believe what he saw.

The place looked like a war zone.

Bodies lay everywhere in pools of blood. Blood splattered the walls, paintings, and pedestals. The gunpowder smell mixed with the metallic, sweet odor of the blood. A shootout had definitely taken place, but Jake still could not process what exactly had happened. He felt nauseous, but was able to hold his stomach. His mind wanted to run, but his legs would not cooperate. Despite the barrage being imposed on Jake's nervous system, he took a step inside.

He recognized the first body as one of the older gangsters from the deli. He had a gunshot wound in his chest as well as a larger one located squarely between his eyes, which were still wide open as if in a suspended state of surprise. He was slumped against a wall across from the entrance to the small office. Jake wondered if his assailant had surprised him from there. Jake stepped around the man, and proceeded through the small storage room to the gallery.

He could see another body lying partially on its side facing Jake. This body was in a moving uniform, meaning it was one of the mobsters that was doing the job. Jake kneeled before entering the gallery to get a better view of the dead man's face. It was Johnny. His eyes peered back at Jake lifelessly, his mouth partially open. The blood pooled under his shoulder, suggesting to Jake that he had been shot in the torso. His gun lay just out of reach of his open hand, dislodged by the impact of the body hitting the floor. Jake could see other bodies to his right in the gallery, but could not make out who they were in the shadows and dark.

It was as Jake stepped farther into the gallery that he heard the chilling voice.

"You should have stayed in the fucking van."

Jake moved back crouching slightly as he turned towards the voice. There, seated on the floor with legs outstretched and arms by his side was Nicky. He had clearly been through the battle, bloody and bruised, with a look of hate that even the exhaustion of the battle couldn't overcome. Jake felt like he was looking at a demon, with Nicky appearing almost on fire as he sat against the large red door which was glowing from the city lights flooding through the windows.

"No, no, no. You ain't going anywhere," Nicky continued as he strained to raise his gun at Jake with his left hand, "it's my turn."

Jake straightened and stepped back into the gallery space. He was staring at the man whose nose he had broken, starting this living nightmare for Jake. "Well, I guess that the devil has brought me a little present before I go and join him," Nicky said while straining to prop himself up against the metal door.

Jake could now see that the man had been shot in the right shoulder.

"I didn't want any of this," Jake tried to explain.

"Yeah, well that's too damn bad, cause you're gonna get it," Nicky interrupted, menacingly.

Nicky started to bring the gun fully up to take aim at Jake. In the split second before he fired, Jake lunged towards the floor, grabbing Johnny's gun and pointing it at Nicky in one motion.

The two shots rang out simultaneously.

Still hearing the sound of the shots echo in the gallery space, Jake's world went black.

*   *   *

The car horn was the first thing that registered in Jake's mind. Jake struggled to open his eyes as he slowly regained consciousness. Lying on his back he started to lift his hands to his aching head but immediately realized that he was covered with something. Touching his chest and neck, Jake found that he was covered in broken glass. Still groggy from the hard hit of his head on the floor, it took him a second to focus on one of the pieces. The fragment in his hand felt like glass and was a deep blue color. Jake looked around, still confused at his whereabouts. It didn't take long before what had happened came crashing back to him.

He sat up quickly on his elbows, pausing as dizziness almost sent him right back down. The broken glass pieces poured off his chest and neck. As he looked down, he saw broken fragments of all different sizes and colors. Some were clear and flat. Others were colored and curved. Regaining more cognizance, Jake sat up straighter and looked towards the red door where Nicky had been taking aim at him. There, slumped along the floor, was Nicky, now joining the others in a pool of his own blood. Like the others, his eyes were wide and staring at Jake. Jake could still detect a hint of Nicky's rage in the lifeless pupils.

The sequence of events was starting to form in Jake's mind. He recalled seeing Nicky raise his gun. He recalled diving to the floor for Johnny's gun and firing. He recalled hearing two shots. *'My shot must have hit'*, he thought, *'and his must have missed. But he was as point blank as I was, how could he have missed?'* Jake stood and stepped towards the storage room to gain a different perspective of the space.

Surveying the gallery space, Jake couldn't believe the carnage. Despite the tapestry of destruction all around him, what quickly caught his eye was the art pedestal positioned between him and Nicky. Some clear and some colored fragmented glass pieces were still on top of it. Jake scanned other pedestals in the gallery space noticing one with a large yellow and green swirled glass bowl under a cubed clear glass cover, and another completely empty with the glass cover laying shattered on the floor next to it. It immediately all fit. *'His aim was true, but he must have hit the pedestal which redirected the bullet.'*

Suddenly, Jake heard the elevator ding, breaking his focus on what happened. Unsure of the time, he worried that it might be the night security guard arriving and taking the elevator to the third floor to make his rounds. Jake quickly left the gallery, and quietly headed down the back stairs. As he reached the bottom floor he noticed that the back door was closed and the van was gone.

His escape would have to be on foot.

He removed his blood stained coveralls before he left the alley, being careful to bundle them under his arm to avoid any transfer. He would dispose of them away from the gallery and ensure they were not found. As he stepped into the bustling sidewalk, the normalcy of the passing scene further masked his shock of the events that had unfolded. *'That was a hit'*, he thought, *'that could have been me.'* His racing mind stopped suddenly with the realization that he hadn't taken any pictures of the scene. Between all hell breaking loose and the arrival of the security guard he had not even thought of it.

Jake could hear sirens in the distance headed towards the gallery. He now knew that trouble had found him again, only this time the stakes were even higher since Jake had just killed a man. The screaming sirens that were approaching rapidly were the final factor driving his decision. This time he really had to leave.

It was time to go where he could hide best, waiting to manage the fallout from the night.

'First, I have to get Sarah', Jake thought with his next move already decided, *'then, time to head to Pine Grove.'*

28

Jake walked towards Sarah's building with purpose, being careful not to make eye contact with anyone he passed. On his way he ducked into an alley and threw his stained coveralls into a dumpster. Returning to the street he could see Sarah's apartment building in the distance. Sarah was outside on the sidewalk talking to someone blocked from Jake's view. He presumed this was her roommate, and really didn't want this to be their first meeting. Sarah turned and locked her gaze on Jake, so there was no postponing the encounter. She returned a worried look that might have surprised Jake had he not been already dealing with the earlier trauma of the day. She ran to him and threw her arms around him.

"Are you ok?" she asked.

"I'm not sure, Sarah. It was a mess," he replied.

"C'mon, let's go inside and you can walk me through it," she said, releasing her embrace, but holding on to one of his arms and starting towards the door. Sarah lived in the basement of a four story tenement building that was sandwiched in a row of other nearly identical buildings for half of the block.

"But what about your roommate? Wait, where did she go?" Jake asked, noticing that the other person was gone.

"My roommate had other things to do, so it will be fine. C'mon."

The apartment was clean and appeared to have been renovated in the last decade. The apartment included laminate-style wood flooring and drop ceilings throughout, which were in good condition. The overall space was simple, consisting of a larger room that encompassed the living room and a small kitchen space, a single bedroom that contained two single beds and basic furnishings, and a small but functional bathroom. There were minimal decorations, most of which were more for convenience than decor, such as lamps and books. No pictures, posters, vases, or other items that one would expect. The entire place appeared very clean and minimalist. Jake and Sarah settled onto the small loveseat in the living room and Jake filled in Sarah on the events at the gallery.

"Oh my God," gasped Sarah, as Jake finished telling her about the robbery-turned-hit job. "All of them are dead?"

"Yeah, all except for Sonny and whoever he was chasing...I think so."

Sarah bit her bottom lip slightly and looked away from Jake, contemplating all that he had shared. Looking back, she now focused on him again, "I don't know what to say. I'm so sorry Jake." She placed her hand on one of his.

"I killed a man tonight, Sarah," Jake said in a hollow voice, "I actually killed him."

Sarah responded softly, "I know Jake. It's awful for you, but you had no choice."

"We always have a choice, Sarah," a sullen Jake responded, still shaken from the evening.

"Yes, and yours was to defend yourself. He was going to kill you," Sarah replied more directly.

Her resolve surprised Jake some, but he appreciated that she was being strong when he was vulnerable.

"They're gangsters Jake. Professional criminals who prey on and kill people for a living." Sarah had positioned herself to look directly into Jake's eyes. "You are not one of them. You are good, Jake. You said yourself that you were going in to try to help. That is not the same as them. The city was just unfair to you again."

These final statements steadied Jake's resolve some. "Thank you, Sarah. And you're right about this city, too," Jake said, now sitting straighter. "It's time to get out of this place, Sarah, and I want you to come with me."

Sarah waffled only slightly, but quickly replied, "Of course, Jake, that's exactly what we should do. Where are we going?"

"I think it's time for us to go to Vermont. I know the lay of the land so we can hide until things shake out. Plus," he continued, his tone shifting softer slightly, "I need to check on my mother and Red."

Sarah seemed to immediately understand this. Having not been home in years, herself, she knew the pull of family and familiarity in times of trouble.

"Ok then, let's go to Vermont."

After collecting their things and loading them into Jake's backpack, they climbed on the Yamaha and sped off into the night.

*   *   *

The couple drove along the Connecticut River on their way to Vermont. After several hours, Sarah pointed to the next exit sign indicating to Jake to take that exit. After Jake took the exit, she directed him to turn right onto Main Street, and then into a spot called The Riverside Diner. The restaurant had originated as an authentic diner car, but had since added on several times. No longer a greasy spoon, the diner now had a menu that read more like a book. The two sat in a booth along the window that overlooked the parking lot, adjacent to an empty lot, next to the highway which was what actually ran alongside the river.

"Hey kids, where you coming in from on that motorcycle?" the waitress asked.

"Headed up from the city," Jake replied.

"On *that* thing?" the waitress questioned, not waiting for an answer to add her opinion, "That must be a terrible ride, but I guess when you're young it doesn't really matter. They'd be picking up pieces of me if I had to ride that thing that far."

Sarah commented, "It's really not that bad, actually."

"Sure hon, if you say so. So, what can I get you two?" asked the waitress.

They both ordered. Sarah decided on a BLT. Jake went with the tall stack of pancakes. "Breakfast, now?" Sarah commented in a surprised tone.

"Sarah, anytime can be breakfast time as far as I'm concerned," Jake responded in a mock serious tone but with a smile on his face.

They talked as they waited for the food. Eventually Jake got to the question that was burning in his mind. "How do you know about this place?" Jake asked.

"I've been here before," she replied, "my brother and I spent some time up and down the coast before the city."

"This is after you left West Virginia?" Jake followed up.

"Yes," she replied simply. Their drinks arrived, pausing the conversation. After the waitress left, Sarah continued before Jake started asking questions again. "We started in Maryland, then made our way north through Pennsylvania to New York, then through Connecticut. We stayed in smaller towns, but eventually I found the city to be the best location."

"That sounds like quite a journey."

"It was, still is in many ways." Sarah seemed to drift away a little bit after this comment.

"But you've been able to take hold in the city. You know parts of it I would never have ventured into on my own. Plus, you have that sweet waitressing job, without it I never would have met you." Sarah smiled at Jake's attempt at humor. "Is your brother in the city?" Jake ventured.

"I'm not sure, actually," she replied, looking down as she played with her silverware.

"That's kinda sad, but I appreciate you sharing," Jake responded with sincerity, placing his hand on hers. He knew how difficult sharing was for himself as well.

The food arrived, and Jake tore into it like it was his last meal. The aroma and warmth of the food, coupled with the dopamine release as their stomachs filled, gave both of them a much needed boost. In a better mood, Jake decided to shift the conversation and tell Sarah some about Pine Grove. Even though some of the memories had been tainted with what happened to his father and Red, he focused on sharing the good parts because he felt that was what Sarah, and he, needed to hear right then.

He described the beautiful terrain, at first focusing on Mount Smith and Squire Lake. He even got so animated that he unconsciously cranked an imaginary fishing reel as he described some of he and his father's biggest walleye catches. He regaled Sarah with tales of hiking through fields of flowers and of course gave every detail of his sanctuary, the pine grove itself next to the camp. He even told her about the Summer Festival, and the fresh baked pie, talking himself into a slice for dessert that was no comparison to the church's. As he described his home, Sarah listened with adoration at Jake's passion, but also felt some melancholy since she had not been to her hometown in years.

Jake then told her more about his time with Red. Opening up on how he had helped Jake learn to grieve for the loss of his father. How he had finished teaching him what it meant to be your own man, guiding Jake through the lessons that his father was unable to finish. He also shared how Red had been caught in the explosion. "That will be our first stop when I get home. I need to find out his prognosis. I hope that he will forgive me," Jake declared.

"If he's the man you describe," Sarah responded, "I am sure that he will."

"And of course I have to go and see my Mom. I miss her and I know that she misses me. She needs to meet you as well, of course. Both of them do." Sarah smiled at this, taking her turn to reach across the table to take Jake's hand.

Jake was lost in thought. Lost in these images and memories. He felt happy to be returning home, something he wasn't sure he would ever feel again. Sarah could read this in his expression and was happy as well, especially to be going there with him. She was also hopeful that the happiness wouldn't be short-lived, but knew from experience that trouble had a way of finding you if it wanted to badly enough.

29

"Wait, where're you going?!" Sonny called out as he slammed through the fire door and out onto the fire escape. "Stop!" he yelled as he started down the stairs of the fire escape. As he reached the alley he stopped and looked around. It was just him; he was alone. Trying to decide which way to head next, he saw the van still parked against the building. *'There'*, he thought, still oblivious to his own rapid breathing and heavy perspiration from the strain of the debacle in the gallery and his pursuit out of the building. He looked inside the cab of the van first. It was empty except for the blanket over the pistol. *'Where the hell is Jake?'*, he wondered, *'probably ran as soon as the shooting started.'* He next went around to the back of the van and peered in. It was empty too.

'What the hell is goin' on here?', he wondered to himself. He realized his pursuit was over now, and his only option was to put as much distance between himself and the gallery as he could. Climbing into the driver's side of the van, he pulled forward, quickly jumping out to close the doors to the van and building, and drove off. He parked the van in Sean O'Connel's lot, wiping his prints from the steering wheel, shifter, and door handles. He removed his coveralls in the back of the van and left, disposing of the blood-covered evidence behind a Chinese restaurant on his way to the deli.

Even after Sonny had made his way back to the deli he felt a foggy combination of shock and rage. His entire crew was gone. He had not managed to steal anything, so the deaths weren't even worth the price. Sonny now sat alone in the back room in silence drinking Peronis trying to collect his thoughts and analyze the events that had transpired. Despite his best efforts to focus he just kept repeating over and over in his mind, *'what the hell just happened?'*, since he was likely suffering from shock. As he was finishing his fourth beer, the other empties on the table in front of him, he was finally able to calm down enough to start sorting through things.

He remembered leaving and driving over. He remembered Jake disabling the security system, and the four of them heading up to the gallery. *'No issues there.'* He remembered going into the office to look for cash or other valuables while the other guys started in the main gallery. He recalled that he could hear them working in the background, but he was mainly focused on the office. He rummaged through drawers looking for a cash box, but came up with nothing. He unplugged the laptop on the desk and was planning to take it. He was starting to work on removing the security monitors to take those as well when he heard Nicky in the other room, "hey, what are you two doing here, and what's with the police jackets...what the fu..."

"And that's when the shooting started," Sonny could hear himself say out loud.

Now the images that flashed into his mind were more scattered. *'I pulled my gun and ducked behind the desk to protect myself at first, and then Archie filled the doorway. What did that son-of-a-bitch say?'* Sonny thought hard, trying to recall. To help his memory, he finished his beer and opened another while absently standing and starting to pace around the room. *'This is the last time...'*, Sonny strained to recall, *'this is the last time you're screwing up, you stupid bastard.'* He then remembered Archie raising the gun to fire, *'you're done taking this family down.'*

This last statement was a mistake by Archie. It gave Sonny just enough time to raise his own gun and fire first. The shot hit the old gangster in the chest, killing him instantly and knocking him back and to the floor.

Sonny continued his macabre memory trip, recalling the realization he had immediately after shooting Archie, *'he was trying to take us out.'* He next remembered moving to the main gallery space, seeing Johnny's dead body on the floor, as well as that of Dominic to his right. Neither were moving. Looking to his left he saw Nicky perched against the door and bleeding. "Sonny, what the hell?" Nicky had asked.

Sonny then went to Nicky, leaning him forward to see how bad his injuries were. He examined the hole in Nicky's shoulder. Looking at his back he realized that the bullet was still lodged inside. While kneeling with him, out of the corner of his eye Sonny saw someone running through and then out of the gallery. *'Louie!'*, Sonny recalled with shocked realization. *'Where was he going? He was carrying his gun, but he wasn't covered in blood.'* He recalled Nicky asking as well, and his response, "I don't know, but I'm gonna go find out. Keep pressure on this thing, and get out if you can." *'I guess that he couldn't.'*

Sonny then remembered his final act before he left the gallery to chase after Louie, stopping only to put a final bullet into Archie's head, right between his eyes.

*   *   *

Silvio and Sonny had quickly spoken to the widows and the goomahs to ensure their silence through payment and threat. The van had been burned and left for the police to find, any evidence completely destroyed. The security guard had found the scene and called it in, his final act before quitting, likely with years of therapy in his future. The police pushed on Silvio and Sonny, bringing them in for questioning, both individually and together, within 48 hours of the robbery. In the true spirit of their vows of silence, neither man said anything. The police even worked their back channel informants, but to no avail. While the police couldn't believe that Silvio and Sonny didn't know about this job, they had nothing to charge them with so the matter was left unsolved.

The Commission, however, wasn't as forgiving. "We have left you to your territory. We turned away when your grandson disrespected a made guy. Now, we have a slaughter at a robbery all over the papers and not even anything to show for it. Restitution for this will be severe, and your family is done," was the decree that was made. This gutted Silvio emotionally. He could not believe his trusted underboss and consigliere had orchestrated such a reckless move.

As he sat with Sonny in the back of the deli he again asked, "And you don't know anything about this, Sonny?" The old man had taken to asking his grandson this question repeatedly, trying to make sense of what, to him, was completely illogical and the end of the life he knew since he was a boy.

"Nah, I told you, Johnny and I brought this to Arch and he told us 'no'. That's what I told my crew. I still can't believe my guys went against me like that...against us like that." Sonny maintained this response each time he was asked, even though it was a lie.

"Alright, but I just can't believe it," Silvio said, shaking his head as he stood to leave, putting on his black fedora and hanging his long coat over his arm. "I'll see you Sunday at dinner, right?" He embraced Sonny with the other hand, and the men kissed each other on the cheek.

"Yeah, I'll see you then." Sonny watched his grandfather leave, feeling a mix of love and sadness. He resumed his spot at the table, and continued to wrestle with his own feelings. *'I can't tell him the truth. That would kill him for sure.'*

As he contemplated, there was a knock on the door that led to the front portion of the delicatessen.

"Yeah?" Sonny barked out.

"Sorry to bother you, but there are two men here to see you," one of the deli employees conveyed.

"They cops? I've had enough of them," Sonny replied.

"I don't think they're cops. They're both Asian and in nice suits," he replied. "They say that it's very important that you speak to them."

Sonny's curiosity was now cautiously piqued. "Yeah, send them in. Thanks."

The two men entered. They were both dressed in black suits with white shirts. Their silk ties were the same except for color. One man's tie was royal blue, the other brick red. Both were of average build, the man in the blue tie was a few inches taller than the other. The man with the red tie carried a leather satchel. They entered the room and stood in front of Sonny.

"Mr. Amoretti," the man in the blue tie said in a tone that left no doubt that he knew who he was talking to even though he had never met Sonny. "I am Mr. Quan, this is Mr. Yi. We represent Mr. Jiao Chang," he continued.

"Mr. who?" Sonny replied with his usual disposition.

"Mr. Chang," replied Mr. Quan.

"I don't know any Mr. Chang," Sonny rebuffed. "What do you two want and make it quick."

Undeterred, Mr. Quan continued his business, never changing his cadence or demeanor. This annoyed Sonny. "If you do not recognize Mr. Chang by name, perhaps you will recognize him by his business, View art gallery. You are familiar with that Mr. Amoretti?" Sonny's anger spiked almost immediately. "What the hell is this?" he asked, rising out of his seat in an attempt to intimidate the two men. Neither man moved. "There is no need for anger or violence, Mr. Amoretti, please sit. I won't be taking much more of your time." Sonny wasn't prepared for this response. He sat back down, puzzled and paying more attention than before.

"We know the gallery robbery was conducted by your organization," Mr. Quan continued.

"I dunno what you're talking about," Sonny replied, it being an almost conditioned response at this point.

Mr. Quan continued, paying no attention to the statement. "We know the police did not find enough evidence to press charges. We also know the robbery was a complete failure and appears to have been a shootout between your associates." Sonny stared blankly at Mr. Quan trying to maintain his best poker face. Mr. Quan continued, "We inventoried the gallery. One bowl was broken. Several paintings were damaged and stained, and one glass hanging piece was also destroyed. Insurance will cover the cost of those pieces. However, one piece could not be accounted for. A carved, jade statuette of a mythical beast called a bixie."

"I don't know anything about any jade trixie, or whatever you called it," Sonny replied flippantly.

"Mr. Amoretti, this piece, the bixie, does have monetary value, however, the importance to Mr. Chang and his family is far greater."

The talk of money and value re-captured Sonny's attention. "How much we talkin'?" Sonny asked.

"Again, Mr. Amoretti, the monetary value is not important," Mr. Quan replied.

"Oh, Mr. Quan, the monetary value is always important to me," Sonny replied with a snicker.

Mr. Quan continued again without engaging further on the monetary value. "Mr. Chang would like you to get the bixie statuette back. He is confident you will be able to do so."

"Well, good for Mr. Chang," Sonny replied, thick with sarcasm, "but like I said, I have no idea what you're talking about. Besides, if, and I do mean *if,* I had any idea how to find the thing, it would cost you…a lot."

"Mr. Chang is a wealthy man and will pay, but not financially," Mr. Quan replied.

"No good," replied Sonny, now leaning in to look Mr. Quan squarely in the eye indicating that the niceties were over and it was time to resolve their meeting. "Pay up, with real American money, or get the hell out."

Mr. Quan continued calmly, "As I said, we will pay but not financially, and you will find the statue, Mr. Amoretti." As he finished, his partner, Mr. Yi, removed a laptop from the satchel and placed it on the table in front of Sonny. As it powered to life, Mr. Quan explained, "Mr. Chang is a very wise man. He loves his daughter dearly, but realizes most of her ventures are not well thought out. He never trusted the security system that was installed, so he had his own fiber optic micro cameras installed throughout the gallery. The cameras blend seamlessly into the black ceiling, and allow Mr. Chang to keep an eye on things from a distance."

As he finished, a video appeared on the screen. Mr. Yi pushed play, and the three men watched as the scene of Sonny shooting Archie in the back room of the gallery unfolded. Sonny held his breath while he watched it. There, on the screen, was the only evidence that the police would need to lock him up for a long time. More importantly, it was the evidence that would no doubt break his grandfather's heart, forever severing any relationship between the two as well as Sonny's ties with the family.

Sonny understood immediately. "I get it," he said in a defeated voice, "did you see who took the bixie?" Mr. Yi opened a second file, fast forwarded through the scene until they reached a specific point. Pushing play the three men watched as Louie grabbed the bixie and ran out of the gallery. *'No wonder the prick didn't stop running. I bet he was the one who double crossed us. Fucking rat!'*, Sonny thought. "Ok, so I get the statue and these videos disappear. Is that what we're saying here?" Sonny asked.

"That is correct, Mr. Amoretti. Mr. Chang just wants the item returned and this whole matter put behind him and his family."

'I want it put behind my family as well.' "Ok, I'll do it," Sonny said, continuing to think, *'but I have no idea how.'*

30

Jake and Sarah made it to Pine Grove well before morning. The temperature was cool, typical for Fall in northern New England. The leaves were turning, and would light the mountains ablaze in the crisp sunlight of the day. It was before sunrise, the only traffic at this time being delivery trucks and men and women in pickups and SUVs off to work their early morning shifts. Jake's face and hands had been numb for hours, but he could feel the warmth of Sarah's body against his as she held him tightly. He was happy that she was with him.

Jake rode directly to the scout camp. They parked at Red's cabin and went inside. Red's things were still in their place, with tools and some wire scattered on the small workbench as if he were in the middle of a project. Jake worked quickly to start a fire in the small pot-bellied stove. Red had shown him how to do this safely. Jake was careful to open the flue, and then adjust the vent on the bottom of the stove to ensure proper air flow to light a fire. The wood stacked nearby was dry and lit easily. Jake then adjusted the vent until the fire burned slowly but brightly. The small fire quickly heated the belly of the stove, which served its purpose in heating the small cabin.

Jake was anxious to see Red, but knew it was too early to visit. He hoped Red was feeling well enough to tell him about the explosion and what followed. He wondered how much recovery Red had achieved since then. His muscles had no doubt atrophied, and Jake had no idea what effect the explosion and recovery had on his motor skills or speech.

Even so, he needed to see Red. He wanted to share with him what happened in the city, and the trouble that he and Sarah had found themselves in. And he wanted Red to meet Sarah, to see how important she is to him, and for Sarah to see how important Red was as well.

The visit would have to wait, though. Now in the warmth and familiarity of the cabin, the exhaustion of the recent events and the trip north began to set in. He knew Sarah was also tired, and decided that they should get some sleep before heading into town. "Sarah, I'm happy you're here with me," was about all that Jake had the energy to say, pausing after to pull an extra blanket from the locker at the foot of the bed. "You take the bed, and I'll sleep on the floor," Jake continued, laying the blanket on the floor.

Sarah walked over to him, taking his hand in hers while putting her other hand around his neck. She looked deeply into his eyes, and he into hers. "I'm glad I'm here too," she said softly, "and you don't need to sleep on the floor." Jake's energy suddenly perked at the realization of what she was insinuating.

They made their way to the bed holding hands. They undressed each other in the intimate glow of the firelight. The new couple then made love for the first time, falling asleep deeply in each other's arms and allowing the weight of recent events to escape their minds at least for a little while.

*   *   *

Jake awoke after only a few hours of sleep to sunlight flitting into his eyes. He kissed Sarah gently to wake her. "I know it's early, but c'mon, I want to show you something."

Rubbing the sleep out of her eyes she asked, "What?" She didn't wait for an answer to rise, pull on her clothes, and follow Jake out of the cabin. Jake led her by the hand down a path to the edge of the lake. There she saw what Jake was excited to show her. The sun was starring in a brilliant sunrise, casting a dazzling orange against the water and landscape. Mist rose from the water's surface causing Sarah to wrap her arms a little tighter and nestle deeper into Jake, who was standing close behind her. As she lifted her gaze she could see the colored leaves begin to shine like a million small lights, all powered by the growing sun.

Jake extended his arm over her shoulder, pointing off to their right. There stood three deer, a doe and two fawns, that had made their way stealthily to the water's edge. The five stared at each other as if bonded together by the shared experience of the brilliant sunrise. "I never tire of this," Jake whispered, "you never see this in the city." He wrapped his arms around Sarah, and they stood and soaked in the mystical scene.

After the sun had risen fully, Jake finally broke the silence. "I have a few other places I want to show you."

"Can it be after breakfast?" Sarah asked.

Jake laughed hard for the first time in a long while. "Of course, I have a place for that, too." They made their way back to the cabin, and Sarah walked towards the motorcycle. "Oh no, too cold for that thing anymore. We're going to ride in style," Jake said with a sheepish smile. Intrigued, Sarah followed him to another outbuilding with a garage door.

Inside was an ancient, but well cared for Ford F150. The truck exterior was two-tone candy apple red, with a silver metallic stripe along the sides. The truck was basic, with chrome bed rails as the only upgrade feature, now pitted from age and wear. Jake opened the passenger door for Sarah to get in. "My lady, your chariot awaits," he said, dramatically. Sarah laughed and climbed in. "Will this thing even start?" she asked.

"On the first try, no doubt," Jake replied, climbing into the driver's seat. The truck started right away. "I wouldn't expect anything less from Red."

As they approached the main gate of the camp, Jake noticed a light on in the main office. "Hey, I wonder if Derek is here?" Jake wondered out loud.

"Who?" asked Sarah.

"Derek Weston, he was a classmate, and works here at the camp. I thought he was only here in the summers, but maybe he's still around. Think that your appetite would allow me to stop and see?"

"I don't know, my stomach is getting restless. I suppose I can hold out though, especially since you're buying," Sarah responded with a smile.

They pulled into the gravel parking area in front of the main office building. It shared the same brown, rough hued plank exterior as the other buildings in the camp, but was twice the size housing both the office and a small apartment. Jake opened the front door and went in with Sarah right behind him. There was no one in the office, which was decorated with scout flags, pictures of past troops and adventures, and a large map of the camp under the plexiglass covering the main counter. There was also a hanging bell with a sign that read 'Always be prepared...to ring the bell for assistance.' Sarah groaned at the play on the scout motto of 'Be Prepared.'

Jake rang the bell. A voice replied almost immediately, "Be right out." Derek entered the room, and his face immediately lit up when he saw Jake. Derek was about the same height as Jake, but with dark brown hair that was combed with a part on one side. He wasn't in scout attire, but rather wore a Green Mountain Club t-shirt, brown pants, and hiking boots. He was lean and in good shape, and had a huge smile on his face as soon as he recognized Jake.

"Jake, you're back! Where have you been, man?" Derek asked.

"I took a little trip," Jake replied, "had to clear my head and get a little distance, I guess you could say."

"Yeah, that stuff with Red was tough. I heard he's really making progress now, though. Is that why you're back?" At this point, Derek noticed Sarah. Without waiting for Jake's response to his question, he extended his hand to Sarah, introducing himself, "Hi. I'm Derek." Sarah shook his hand and introduced herself. "Great to meet you, Sarah. Jake is a great guy, just great. You got yourself a good one there, Sarah," Derek added with an enthusiastic rhythm to his words.

Derek continued without pause, "So, you going to visit Red? He's over at Apple Rehab."

"Yeah, we're headed over there after breakfast, I think. I want to stop and visit Mom as well. What are you still doing here, Derek?"

"I work here full time now. I run the office year-round. I've been trying to keep up with the maintenance as well while Red is down, but there is still a lot to do before winter. Hey, now that you're here, you want to help out? We can try to set you up in a different cabin since I'm sure that you won't want to stay in Red's. If you're sticking around, of course."

"Actually, that sounds pretty good, Derek, thanks. I'll give it some thought and get back to you, if that's ok?"

"Of course, no problem. You'd be helping me out, for sure," Derek added for good measure.

They said their goodbyes, and Jake and Sarah headed out. They drove to town and stopped to eat at a local spot called The Blue Heron. The place was full of both locals and leaf peepers, but they were able to find a few stools at the counter.

"This place has been here as long as I can remember," Jake said, "the older couple who own the place still runs it. Their daughter was my babysitter when I was little. It still amazes me how everyone seems to know everyone else somehow. Typical small town, I guess."

"I know that world, too, all too well. Sometimes good and sometimes bad," Sarah responded, quickly shifting to what she was going to order for her long awaited breakfast.

"So, what's the specialty of the house, moussaka?" she joked.

"Ha, no. The lumberjack stack of pancakes is my favorite."

"Pancakes again?" Sarah asked, her voice pitching higher with disbelief.

"You can never have too many pancakes," Jake replied, rubbing his stomach. They placed their order and waited, talking and enjoying the energy and community of the restaurant.

After they filled their bellies, they stopped to buy a card and flowers at Sarah's behest. "He is going to hate that," Jake argued to no avail, "You'll see." They then made their way to Apple Rehab to visit Red.

The single story center was just outside of town. Jake and Sarah signed in and made their way down the main hallway to Red's room. Jake paused outside the room for a second, unsure of what to expect seeing his friend and mentor for the first time after the accident. Sarah took his hand, saying simply, "it will be ok." Jake took a deep breath, fully pushed open the half shut door, and walked inside, with Sarah just behind him. Red was sitting in a chair next to his bed by the window. He was reading, dressed in sweatpants with a flannel shirt, and was neatly groomed. He looked at Jake, and Jake at him.

Red spoke first.

"Well, it's about time," Red said in as sarcastic a tone as he could muster with a sly smile on his face.

'Of course, I shouldn't have expected anything else', Jake thought to himself. "Hi Red," Jake said with a smile and sheer relief at the man's opening, "Yeah, sorry. I've been busy, I guess you could say."

Red shifted his attention to Sarah. "Wait, don't tell me, you actually managed to get a woman to like you?" Red asked in a mocking voice. "If that's true, maybe she should be getting her head checked instead of mine."

Jake quickly intervened to stop the mock verbal assault. "Alright, I suppose I deserve this abuse, but not her. She hasn't done anything," Jake replied with his smile still set across his face.

"Hello Red, I'm Sarah," Sarah offered, "I've heard so much about you, it's nice to finally meet you. These are for you." Sarah handed Red the flowers and card.

"Hi Sarah, and thank you," Red responded with the best sincerity that he could muster.

"See, I told you he'd hate those," Jake commented.

Red looked at Jake and then to Sarah, "Sarah, except for your choice in men, you seem like a nice person, so I'm warning you not to believe a single word he says about me. It's all untrue or overly exaggerated, I'm sure."

Mark Raymond

"Well, you two better sit down, I want to hear what you've been up to." Red motioned to the two guest chairs, one of which was for the other bed in the room which did not have a tenant at present. Jake filled Red in on his move to the city, on the restaurant, finding the book, and his success at cooking. He told him about the times he and Sarah had done some exploring in the city, as well as their trip to Pennsylvania on the Yamaha. He even told Red about the art gallery and his 'side job' installing the security system. He did not tell Red about the Mob or his involvement in the robbery gone bad, or that they may be on the run.

"Must have been a damn cold ride up here on that bike," was Red's first comment.

Jake expected this type of response from him, *'Focused on the motorcycle ride of all things, he never changes'*, Jake thought. "Yeah, it was pretty cold, but Sarah kept me warm," Jake replied looking at Sarah.

"And where are you staying?" Red asked.

"In your cabin, although Derek offered me a job catching up on the maintenance until you're back on your feet. How are you making out by the way?" Jake asked.

"First," Red responded, "get your own cabin, and don't mess up my stuff too much. I have a very specific organizational system, you see Sarah," he joked. "Second, me, I'm practically fine. They say I should be out of here soon. Of course they've been saying that for several weeks since I got the brace off. Guess an old man like me takes longer to heal than when I was a punk kid like you."

"What happened, Red?" Jake asked with a serious tone.

"Well, stupidity Jake," Red replied matter-of-factly, "I should have checked the cabin before I started working. My sniffer hasn't worked so well since my time in the Navy, so I

175

didn't even smell the gas. That explosion blew me clear across the path. If I had been further inside the cabin I would have been dead." After a short pause, Red continued, "I suffered a skull fracture as well as a burst fracture of my C7 vertebrae. Because of the skull fracture they held off on surgery for my back. At the time I didn't have use of my legs, and they feared that I had suffered an incomplete spinal cord injury, or partial tear of my spinal cord."

Jake visually tensed at this last sentence, even though he knew that Red was undergoing physical therapy. "It ends up, however, that it was spinal cord shock caused by the trauma and swelling that resulted in paralysis, not a tear. After the swelling went down and my skull fracture healed enough, they fitted me in a back brace for several weeks. I got that off a few weeks ago, and have been going through physical therapy to get my strength and balance back. My therapist actually tells me that I am doing real well, Jake. The doctors all say that it's a miracle that I survived. Whatever, I'll take it."

Tears filled Jake's eyes. Tears of relief for Red, tears of relief for himself and finally being able to come back and see Red, and most importantly tears of relief that Red hadn't left him either through death or paralysis. "I'm so happy that you're alive, Red. I couldn't take it if...if..." Jake's statement trailed off.

"I told you, I'm not going anywhere, Jake, I'm here to help you no matter what."

"I know," Jake responded, regaining his composure.

Shifting the topic, Red asked, "You been out to visit your mom yet? I know that she misses you."

"Not, yet. We're heading there later though, I promise," Jake replied. "I didn't call her enough…," Jake added, trailing off.

"That sounds good, and don't you worry, she'll just be happy to have you home. Ok, now you've gone and wore me out. I need to rest before that old nurse Betty comes in here and harasses me again. I secretly think she likes me, but she'll never admit it. Come back and see me, ok, and don't be moving any of my stuff, you got it?"

"Yeah, I got it," Jake responded, standing.

Sarah didn't say anything as the men had talked, but she rose with Jake, walked over to Red, and gave the man a hug being careful not to squeeze too tightly. "Thank you for taking care of Jake, Red," she whispered.

"You too," Red replied, softly, "you too."

31

Mr. Quan and Mr. Yi had left Sonny in the back room of the delicatessen. Sonny knew that he had no choice but to find the bixie statue and return it to Mr. Chang. *'They have me dead to rights on that video!'*, Sonny thought, slamming his fist on the table. *'I gotta think, how am I going to find Louie?'* He called Louie's cell phone several times with no answer. *'Of course not, freakin' prick.'* He played back his relationship with Louie in his mind, including trying to recall how they were first introduced only a few years ago. Louie wasn't on Sonny's radar at the time, but few petty criminals were.

He struggled to recall how Louie had even ended up on his crew. He knew he was a decent earner, and he clearly recalled the two times he had helped them access a few jewelry stores. "Both Johnny and Nicky had vouched for the guy as an earner," he recalled out loud, referring to the requirement that two made guys vouch for someone new. This rule was put in place after undercover FBI agent Joe Pistone was promoted to made guy under the name Donnie Brasco, having only been vouched for by one made guy, Mob captain Dominick "Sonny Black" Napolitano. *'But Johnny and Nicky hadn't tried to get Louie made, they just vouched for his value as an associate'*, he further recalled.

Louie just seemed to be around, gradually earning their trust and working his way into the crew. *'Pretty damn savvy, gotta admit. Survivor mentality'*, Sonny thought, *'and never any trouble either. What the hell is going on here?'*

Sonny spent the next day asking around the neighborhood to see if anyone knew Louie's whereabouts, but all inquiries came up empty. Several people said they hadn't seen him around, while a few thought they might have, but couldn't be sure. *'This is useless. No one knows nothin', and I don't even have my crew around to consult. Even Jake is gone.'* Sonny's next thought shot into his mind like an electric shock. *'I bet he's with Jake.'* Sonny tried dialing Jake on the burner phone that they had given him. There was no answer. After trying two more times with the same result he stopped trying, and focused on figuring out his next move. *'I bet that little girlfriend of his at the restaurant will know where he is.'*

Without hesitation Sonny headed out the back door of the deli and straight to The Athena. Entering, he made a beeline for the kitchen ignoring anyone in the front. Deniz was back, busily cooking with Pedro assisting with prep. "Where's Jake?" Sonny asked without any introduction. Pedro looked cautiously at Deniz who nodded at him indicating that he should leave the kitchen quickly. "I asked a question," Sonny barked, impatience evident in his face and tense features.

"I do not know," Deniz replied calmly, trying to mask his nervousness.

"Well, what about that little girl that he's with? Where is she?" Sonny asked.

By this time Zehab had made his way into the kitchen. He instantly recognized Sonny from their meeting at the deli, and quickly chose to temper his normal confrontational response. "Hello. Who are you looking for?" Zehab asked.

"I'm looking for Jake, but this guy says that he's not here, so I'm looking for his little girlfriend. The waitress. You know the one."

"Yes, I know the one, but neither of them are here. I haven't seen them for a few days. Neither has my cousin here," Zehab responded.

"You wouldn't be protecting them would ya?" Sonny questioned, paying close attention for any tells from the two cousins, "Because I'm sure that you aren't looking for any more problems, right Zehab?"

Zehab was surprised that Sonny had actually remembered his name. "Protect them. No!" Zehab responded resolutely, "They abandoned me! Thankfully my cousin here came back and brought his daughter to cover the front. My cousin is an honorable man and friend." Zehab put his hand on his cousin's shoulder as he finished his sentence to emphasize their restored partnership.

"Well, I gotta find this kid. You got any idea where he went?" Sonny continued.

"I do not know. Neither of them told me anything, they just left," Zehab responded.

"Well, do you know anything about him? Where he lives, where he's from? Where she's from?" Sonny asked, growing even more impatient.

"The only thing that I know is that he was from Vermont. Pine Town, or Grove City or something. Pine Grove, that's it," Zehab said, recalling what Jake had told him.

"Yeah, he said that he worked at a scout camp up there where he learned to work in the kitchen and do repairs and stuff," Deniz added, recalling their first encounter.

"And what about the girl, do you know where she's from?" Sonny asked. "No, I do not," Zehab replied, looking over at Deniz who was shaking his head indicating he didn't know either.

Sonny's jaw tightened to contain his growing frustration at the situation. "Well, I guess I'm going to Vermont."

32

Jake and Sarah left the rehab facility and headed to his mother's house. On the way Sarah asked, "Why didn't you tell Red about the robbery and the Mafia?"

"I just couldn't," Jake replied, "after all that he has been through. Plus, I need to take care of this myself. I shouldn't need to fall back on Red or anyone else to take care of my mess."

"I know, but he seems great, Jake. You're lucky to have someone like him you can rely on for help when you need it. And I think that we may end up needing it," Sarah replied.

"I know Sarah, but I need to be my own man. I promised that I would finish that job and we would move on. That's what we're doing. No looking back." Sarah could sense that the discussion was over for now, and she didn't want to push harder and risk ruining Jake's reunion with his mother.

They arrived at Jake's house, pulling Red's truck to a stop in front of the house. The house was a modest craftsman style, two floors with a peaked dormer in the front over the porch that stretched the entire length of the house. The cedar shake shingles were faded, as was the white of the trim, but both were still in good condition. Jake and Sarah walked up the concrete walkway and porch stairs and knocked on the door. As Jake's mother, Mary, opened the door a huge smile spread across her face. Jake barely had time to get the words "Hi Mom" out of his mouth before Mary had risen up on her tiptoes and wrapped her arms around her son's shoulders in a loving embrace.

"Thank God you're home," Mary said as she held her son with tears of happiness and relief in her eyes.

After this initial reunion, she turned her attention to Sarah. "Jake, who is this?" she asked.

"Mom, I want you to meet Sarah. She's my girlfriend." Jake replied, looking at Sarah and smiling at his introducing her this way for the first time.

Sarah smiled back. "Oh Jake, she's beautiful," his mother gushed, making Sarah blush slightly. "Well, come in dears. I want to hear about everything," she continued, taking Sarah by the arm and leading her inside. Jake followed, a little embarrassed, but mostly relieved, by his mother's warm welcome.

Inside things looked the same as when he left. His father's chair was still in its place in the living room, and even though he was gone his presence was still in the air. His mother had obviously been cooking, and had pots boiling on the stove in the kitchen which was open to the living room. The familiar smell wafted into his nostrils, instantly bringing him back to simpler times when his entire family shared the meal of chicken pot pie made from scratch. Jake's reminiscence was only broken by the laughter emanating from the kitchen. Sarah and his mother were getting on like old friends as they finished preparing the meal. Jake popped his head into the kitchen, "You two ok in here for a bit?"

"We are just fine, aren't we dear?" his mother replied.

Sarah looked at him, smiling, "We are indeed," she added for good measure.

Jake smiled contentedly at the two most important women in his life, with relief and love flooding his senses. Suddenly and solemnly, Jake blurted, "Mom, I'm sorry," as the waves of recent emotion poured out in one quick statement. His mother stopped her work, putting down the knife that she was using to cut vegetables, and focusing all of her attention on Jake. "I'm sorry that I left like I did. I'm sorry that I left you behind. That wasn't right," Jake continued.

"Jake," his mother said, caringly walking to her son, "there is no right or wrong with death. There were plenty of times I considered leaving myself after your father died. Plus, for you...Red's accident. I knew you were hurting, and as hard as it was to see you go I knew a change of scenery might have been exactly what you needed." She took Jake's hand, "Besides, you're home now, safe and sound. That's all that a mother really wants, to see her boy safe and sound and happy". She looked at Sarah smiling, and then back at Jake.

"I love you, Mom. Thank you for being the person that you are in my life. I can't imagine things without you."

"Aww, Jakey, I love you too wherever you roam." Sarah looked on with admiration for Jake and his mother, and the bond they still shared even after all of the recent trauma in their lives. "Ok," his mother proclaimed, first brushing her apron flat, and then the tears from her eyes, "well you'd better let Sarah and I get back to it or things won't be ready for dinner."

Jake left the kitchen still emotional, but wanting to give the two women some more time to get to know each other. He headed outside for some fresh air, and walked into the backyard. He went through the gate of the chain link fence into the small yard, looking back through the picture window into the kitchen where his mother and Sarah were working together. Smiling with satisfaction at their harmony, he headed to his father's shed in the back corner of the lot. While he had been in and out of the shed in the summer to get the lawn mower, he always made his time in the shed as purposeful and quick as possible.

Jake removed the padlock, which was never actually locked but more for show, and stepped inside. The mustiness of the space mixed with the smell of wood and old motor oil created an aroma unique to the little shed. Jake marveled at the tools, each in its specific place, as well as the 12-guage pump shotgun hanging on the wall. The open boxes of buckshot and slugs sat on the small workbench beneath the gun. There were gardening tools, the push lawn mower, and various boxes of spare fasteners, tools, and other hardware throughout.

Jake soaked it all in. He had never faced this aspect of his mourning, but he didn't feel the pain he had expected. Rather, he felt a fond warmth for his father. He also reflected on the similarities between his father and Red. Both good men who worked hard and loved those close to them, willing to do anything to keep them safe and sound. Both willing to teach and let loved ones fail in the spirit of growth and learning. Both taking great pride in handling their business. Jake had come to value these characteristics as he matured into a man.

While only early afternoon, Jake, Sarah, and Mary sat together at the family's dinner table and enjoyed the hot pot pie. Without Jake's father there to temper his wife's curiosity, Mary asked what seemed like an endless stream of questions about Jake's time in the city. Jake tactfully filled her in on the sights and sounds, the restaurant, and how he met Sarah, being careful not to include any details on his interaction with the Amoretti family or the art gallery. As with Red, he had no intention of bringing this trouble to her front door.

"Mom, I think that I'm going to visit Dad's grave tomorrow. Do you want to come along?" Jake asked after he had finished two helpings of pot pie as well as some homemade banana bread.

"Oh Jakey, I appreciate it but I think that you should take Sarah yourself. You can take the hand trimmers and cut back any grass, though, if you don't mind. Unless you're heading somewhere else soon," she tactfully replied, fishing for Jake and Sarah's plans.

Jake chuckled at his mother's obvious inquiry, "Sure Mom, I'll take them and bring them back."

"Well, that would just be wonderful," his mother replied with a smile.

33

Sonny headed north out of the city. He took I-95 North and then exited onto I-91 North in Connecticut, continuing through Massachusetts until he reached the Vermont border. Stopping to stretch his legs and use the facilities he entered Pine Grove into his GPS unit. The directions continued on I-91 North eventually shifting to secondary roads that lead him to the hamlet. It was late when he arrived, so he stopped at the Sugar Maple Inn, the first place he found with a vacancy sign. The inn was an old three story house with a large porch, high gables, and overtly designed in Victorian style, including intricate trim around each of the gables. It was painted light maroon with darker trim, and was clearly well maintained. Sonny paid no attention to the exterior of the inn other than locating the entrance after he parked.

Inside he was greeted by a large living space filled with overstuffed furniture and an overabundance of tables crammed with trinkets and pictures. A fireplace in the corner of the room was ablaze and a white Persian cat was sleeping in front of it. "Look at all of this crap," Sonny commented, finally paying attention to the inn's decor.

"Crap to some, treasures to others, my dear," came the response from the elderly owner of the inn. Margaret Conley had inherited the house from her parents years prior. She and her deceased husband Frank restored the place in their favorite era, then decided to open the house to others as an inn. Sonny hadn't noticed her at the back of the hall when he entered.

"Uh, yeah, sorry about that. So, you have a room I can rent?" Sonny asked.

"Yes dear, third floor though, is that going to be a problem?"

"No, that's fine. Anywhere to eat around here?" he further inquired.

"Well, I'm not sure of anything this late, but you are welcome to fix yourself a sandwich if that will work. Also, we include breakfast in the rate as well. Tomorrow is Belgian waffles."

'Nothing open? Where the hell am I?', Sonny wondered to himself.

After he paid and fixed himself a turkey and ham sandwich he walked upstairs to his room. It contained a brass bed with a homemade quilt, a few side tables with antique lamps, a small tv mounted to one wall, and a few other shelves packed with more nick-nacks. Sonny barely noticed. He laid on the bed thinking about Louie and Jake. He had convinced himself on the drive up that they had been in on the double-cross.

He also thought of the many ways that he wanted to kill Louie and Jake when he got his hands on them.

*　　　*　　　*

The next morning after his Belgian waffle, which he ate in his room to avoid any of the other guests, he headed off to the scout camp. Mrs. Conley gave him directions and he made his way out of town towards Camp Megeso. When he arrived he pulled into the parking area in front of the main office building and went inside. Derek, who was working inside, looked up with surprise, immediately noticing that Sonny was not dressed like his typical visitor.

Quickly recovering, Derek smiled his best welcoming smile while walking over to greet Sonny at the counter. "Hi. How's it going? How can I help you?" he asked.

"Yeah, hey," replied Sonny as he took in Derek's brown cargo pants, heavy hiking boots, thick fleece, and skull hat. "I'm looking for Jake, is he here?" he asked.

Masking his suspicion, Derek replied, "Um, no, he's not."

"Has he been here?" Sonny continued inquiring.

"Mind if I ask how you know Jake?" Derek probed.

"Actually, I do mind," Sonny responded curtly, but quickly regained his composure. "Sorry kid, been a long trip. My name's Johnny," he lied, "I worked with him in the city. I'm on my way north and thought I'd surprise him."

Derek hesitated for a beat while sizing up Sonny.

"Look, I told you I worked with him at the restaurant. He told me all about Pine Grove and working at the camp and learning to repair stuff up here. Can't you help me out? It's not like I'm going to hurt him or anything, we're just friends." *'I can't believe I said I'm not going to hurt him, Jesus Sonny get it together'*, he thought, scolding himself. He tried to smile his smoothest smile to mask his mistake.

After a second Derek finally replied, "Well, he isn't here. Last I knew he went in to see Red."

"Red, right, I remember Jake talking about him. He taught him how to repair stuff, right?" Sonny offered.

Still wary, Derek had to admit that it seemed like Sonny knew Jake.

"Yeah, that's him. He's the maintenance guy here, but he had an accident. He's in a rehab facility now."

"Oh, that's terrible," Sonny said feigning concern, "is he going to be ok?"

"Yeah, he had a rough time of it, but he is getting better," Derek replied.

"Can you tell me which one? I'm just passing through so I don't have a lot of time. Maybe I can catch Jake there before I have to move on."

"Apple Rehab," Derek replied hesitantly. "Thanks kid, you have no idea how much I appreciate that," Sonny said, smiling again.

Sonny turned and headed out of the office. Derek reflected on the conversation and decided to call Red to let him know that Sonny may be on his way to find Jake. Red wasn't in his room so Derek left a message and, although a bit distracted, went back to his work.

Again using his GPS, Sonny arrived at his destination, Apple Rehab. After signing in he headed to Red's room, number 213. As he walked by other residents, most of whom were seniors, he thought about his grandfather whose heart was still completely broken at the loss of his Mafia brothers, friends, and identity. Sonny honestly wasn't sure how the trauma of this loss would play out for him. '*Early grave, long lonely existence, ending up in a place worse than this?*' Sonny pushed the thoughts out of his head and steadied his resolve to get the statuette back to Mr. Chang so that he could at least be around for his grandfather.

Sonny arrived at room 213 and paused outside the doorway. It was silent inside. He quickly poked his head in, but didn't see anyone. Entering the room, he confirmed that it was empty. "Well, great," Sonny mumbled to himself. "I drive all the way up here and the freakin' guy isn't even here." Sonny decided to look through Red's stuff for any possible information. In his drawers he found a few cards that people had sent, as well as an ancient watch and some other personal effects. In the closet he found some clothes, but nothing that he could use. Frustrated, he turned his attention to the small counter next to the closet. A bouquet of fresh flowers and a card sat on the counter.

Sonny picked up the card, reading the signatures inside: 'Hope that you feel better soon, Jake and Sarah'. "So Sarah is with Jake and Louie as well. This is going to be easier than I thought. Take out my crew? I'll be taking yours out as well, all three of you," Sonny said out loud in a threatening tone while he crushed the card in his hand and threw it down on the counter, his plan forming quickly in his mind. "I'm done chasing you kid," he continued, "it's time to bring you to me."

Sonny turned and strode with purpose out of the room, almost walking right into a man sleeping in a wheelchair in the hall. "Watch it old timer," Sonny barked as he rushed past.

Red kept his eyes shut until the man was out of the hallway. He had been returning to his room when he saw Sonny enter, and had heard the entire thing. Acting quickly, he took advantage of an empty wheelchair in the hallway, and the fact that Sonny had never seen him before, to hide in plain sight outside of his room. As he rose from the chair he continued to look down the hall wondering, '*Jake, what have you gotten yourself into?*'

Sonny stopped at the counter on his way out of the facility. The woman who had checked him in was not there. Sonny leaned over the counter and studied the binders located on the side of the desk. Removing the one labeled 'guest log' he turned to the previous day. He quickly found what he was looking for. Written in the entry log was one person with the first name of Jake: Jake Cleary. '*Ok, Jake Cleary, I'm coming for you*', he thought. After returning the binder, and a quick search in the phone book sitting on the desk, Sonny was on his way.

Sonny pulled his SUV along the curb a few houses down from the two-story craftsman style house. He made his way to the front door and knocked. Jake's mother, Mary, answered. "Yes?" she asked cautiously.

"Hello, I'm a friend of Jake's. Is he here?" Sonny asked.

"A friend of Jake's?" his mother asked, "Um no, he isn't. What was your name? I'll tell him that you stopped."

"My name is Johnny, ma'am," Sonny lied, "I'm sorry but that won't do, see I'm only passing through town and was hoping to catch him. Do you know where he is?"

His mother's suspicion grew quickly and all that she wanted to do was shut and lock the door. "No, I don't. Now I think that you better go. I'll tell him that you stopped, Johnny," she replied, starting to shut the door.

Sonny slammed his hand against the closing door. "I don't think so," he threatened. He then pulled the pistol from his waistband, pointing it at Mary, and forcing his way in. "Alright, guess we're gonna do this the hard way, now get in there."

34

Jake parked the old Ford at the head of the path that wound down to the section of the cemetery where his father was buried. He and Sarah made their way to his father's grave, Jake holding Sarah's hand. Sarah marveled at the beautiful spot on the hill overlooking the town below. They proceeded past the stones of various ages and wear to the fresh granite headstone of Jake's father.

"Dad, this is Sarah," Jake said straightaway. "I wish that you could meet her in person, but I guess this will have to do. She's great. I met her in the city. We checked out all kinds of great places down there, and work together at a restaurant. I'm actually the head cook, if you can believe that," he continued in the manner of a son looking for the approval of his father. "Mom met her, and really likes her too," he then added for good measure.

After this statement Jake let go of Sarah's hand, taking a step closer to the headstone and touching the top of it lightly as he breathed deeply to maintain his composure. "Dad, I got into some trouble down there," Jake confessed, surprising Sarah. "I didn't mean for it to happen. I was trying to do the right thing, what you and Red have taught me. I was trying to protect someone that I love. But…things just blew up. But we're safe now, Dad, I'm done with that mess. We left and are starting things over again away from danger." Jake looked at Sarah, continuing, "and the person that I love is safe."

The sudden ring of the burner cell in Jake's pocket invaded the moment. Looking at the display Jake was surprised that it was his mother's phone number. Jake showed it to Sarah chuckling, "we haven't even been gone that long and she is already calling. Probably wants to hang out with you some more."

Sarah's face dropped. "Jake, how did your mother get that number?" she asked, knowing that the phone was a burner that the mobsters had given him.

Jake's wind left him as the weight of Sarah's question sank in. "Hello?" he asked trepidatiously.

"Hello Jake," the voice on the other end replied. Jake froze in terror. It wasn't his mother's voice, but he recognized it immediately. It was Sonny Amoretti's. "We need to talk, kid. I think it's time you came and visited your mother."

35

Marvin Filmer burst into the New York City police precinct. "I saw someone, I saw someone...red hair, red hair," he stammered at the police officer working the desk.

"Marvin, now what are you doing in here?" Sergeant Deion Davis, asked, surprised. The entire neighborhood police force knew of Marvin, a conspiracy theorist who carried a worn copy of George Orwell's book '1984' everywhere he went, and never failed to quote it to anyone who would listen. Unfortunately for Marvin he would also quote it to people who did not want to listen, resulting at times in intervention by the police to stop his harassment. Otherwise considered harmless, Sergeant Davis was surprised to see him in a police station, especially since Marvin referred to the police as 'the henchmen of Big Brother'.

"I saw someone. I saw someone!" Marvin yelled at the Sergeant.

"Slow down, Marvin," Sergeant Davis responded, "take your time and start at the beginning. Who did you see?"

"I don't know him, but he had red hair, he was leaving," Marvin continued at a more normal volume.

"Leaving where, Marvin?" Sergeant Davis asked.

"The alley. He left the alley," Marvin added.

"Ok, you saw someone...," Sergeant Davis started.

"A man, it was a man," interrupted Marvin.

"Ok, ok...you saw a man leave an alley," Sergeant Davis summarized before again being interrupted by Marvin. "With red hair, the man had red hair."

Marvin nodded profusely at the correct statement.

"Right," Sergeant Davis responded slowly while sitting back in his chair. "Marvin, there is no law against a man with any color hair leaving an alley," he instructed, "now why don't you go on your way, we have real crimes to look into." Marvin stayed put, mumbling to himself while he sat on the bench under the watchful eye of the desk Sergeant. Marvin sat for quite a while, when suddenly he burst out, starting again where he had left off earlier, "It was the alley behind the old phone building...where the shooting happened."

Sergeant Davis looked skeptically at Marvin, having almost forgotten that he was there. "Shooting, what are you talking about Marv?" he asked with a skeptical tone.

"I was walking and I hear shots in the old phone building. I waited to see if you guys were going to show up, but you didn't. I walked to the front of the building to see if you guys were there, but you weren't. Then I walked to the back and saw a man leaving with red hair. Red hair!"

Marvin's eyes were wide as he finished his explanation. It was the longest continuous thing that Sergeant Davis had ever heard out of the man other than his non-stop conspiracy babble. Before Sergeant Davis could respond again a call came in over the computer-aided dispatch system, *10-39 reported...* "Is that it?" Marvin exclaimed. Sergeant Davis quickly shushed him, waving his hand at him to be quiet, but unable to hear the location due to Marvin's interruption. The Sergeant leaned closer to the speaker...*multiple casualties. Request multiple units respond to secure the scene.*

Sergeant Davis pointed at Marvin, non-verbally commanding him to wait, and then picked up the phone and made a call. Once done with his call he returned the receiver to the ancient black phone that sat on his desk. "Looks like you were telling the truth Marvin. That was a call for a burglary at the old phone building where shots were evidently fired. So, just sit tight. Detective Doyle will be out to take your statement."

*   *   *

A few days after Marvin burst into the Precinct, the arrest was quick and without drama. The detainee's red hair was mussed, but burning like a torch to the eyes of the police officers sent for the arrest. Even though compliant, the detainee himself, Sean O'Connell, was very confused.

"What did I do?" Sean asked for the third time as the officers were guiding him into the back seat of the cruiser.

"C'mon Sean, you know what you did," replied one of the officers.

"I don't have any idea why you all are harassing me," Sean replied evenly. This wasn't Sean's first arrest, and remaining calm was his conditioned response to the situation.

"You know damn well why we're pinching you, Sean. Another security system hit? C'mon, it hasn't been that long since last time. I thought you were smarter than that," the officer added.

"Sorry lads, whatever this is, it ain't me," Sean replied, positioning himself in the back seat.

"Yeah, well someone thinks they have enough to say it *is* you," the officer emphasized. Before waiting for a response, the officer continued, "Sean O'Connell, you're under arrest for first degree burglary, murder, and probably a whole ton of other charges, you prick. You have the right to remain silent. Anything you say can and will be used against you in a court of law…"

Sean was too shocked to keep paying attention. He had been busted in the past for burglary and other lesser crimes, but never committed murder or had even been involved in anything that came close. "Hey, I don't know what's going down, but I definitely didn't murder someone," Sean pleaded from the backseat as they drove to the precinct.

"Save it for the detectives, Sean, but you're screwed," the second officer replied with a snort.

When they arrived at the precinct Sean was taken directly to an interrogation room. He was seated in an orange plastic chair and his handcuffs were locked to a small gray table. There were two additional orange chairs on the other side of the table. The walls of the room were dirty white with stained drop ceiling tiles and an ancient, tiled floor. With the exception of a camera mounted in one of the corners, the room was completely bare.

After an hour, two men entered the room. "I don't know how you did it, Sean, but you got yourself in a pile of shit," the first man through the door announced. Sean's instincts to remain calm had kicked back in as he sat silently trying to maintain a steady look and not offer any information that could be incriminating. The first man knew of Sean, and his loose affiliation with the Amoretti crime family. He did not expect him to be very compliant so he just continued, "I'm Detective Doyle, this is my partner Detective Williams."

Detective Doyle was Irish just like Sean, but hadn't grown up in the neighborhood. He was short with a solid build. His neck strained at his unbuttoned shirt collar, and his flat end tie was a few years out of style. His partner had dark skin, was lean and muscular in build, and wore a gray suit, starched shirt and stylish tie. Detective Williams grew up two neighborhoods over, and went to college on a swimming scholarship, which he continued to do for exercise.

"How did you get yourself into this mess, Sean?" Detective Doyle asked. Detective Williams just stood in the corner of the room with his arms folded, holding a manilla envelope in his left hand, evidently the 'bad cop' for this interrogation. Sean remained silent, so Detective Doyle continued, "I thought you were tight with the Amoretti's, what happened, they kill your mother or something, Jesus?" The shock factor of this question made the impact that Detective Doyle had hoped for. While Sean still didn't reply, he couldn't completely conceal the concern creeping on to his face. "Bad, bad, bad Sean. They're gonna skin you alive for this one," Detective Doyle continued, shaking his head.

Sean couldn't hold his tongue any longer, "What are you going on about?"

"You know, Sean, the art gallery," Detective Doyle carefully responded, trying not to show his entire hand.

"You mean the robbery? I didn't have anything to do with that. You guys got nothin'," he said confidently.

"Nothing?" replied Detective Doyle, "I got a witness." He let this revelation hang in the air for effect.

"Who?" Sean asked.

"Oh no, Sean, that's not how this works. You know better. I tell you something, you tell me something. Isn't that how it works Detective Williams?" Detective Doyle asked, looking back at his partner.

"That's how it works," Detective Williams replied evenly in his baritone voice, continuing to stare at Sean.

Sean contemplated his next response. His experience told him to either keep quiet or lawyer up, but the murder charge still had him rattled. "I see you thinking, Sean. Stay quiet?

Lawyer up? I know how you mobsters track. See, the thing is you know that we can make this thing stick. A witness, plus your past jobs…it all aligns so *beautifully*," Detective Doyle emphasized by kissing his fingertips, the Italian chef's kiss gesture. The reference to the Italians was not lost on Sean.

After a few seconds Sean decided to give a little more information to hopefully get more in return so that he could actually understand the situation. "I didn't do anything at any art gallery," Sean said.

"Are we really doing this again, Sean?" Detective Williams interjected sternly, "Screw this, let's let him out and let the Mob have at him."

"Wait!" Sean quickly said, "What I was going to say is that I didn't do anything in the gallery, but I did help them out in setting up the robbery. That's it."

Detective Doyle again took over the questioning, "Good, Sean, you're starting to see how this works. Gonna need a little more though, how did you help them set it up?"

"I set up some kid that was working with them to do a security system install at the place. Got him the gear, then walked him through it and how to install it. I also loaned them a van. That's it," Sean replied, "They ain't going to skin me alive for that."

"No, but they will for this," Detective Williams said, stepping closer to the table and throwing the manilla folder down in front of Sean. "Open it. Take a good look," Detective Williams continued, menacingly.

Sean struggled to open the envelope with the cuffs on his hands. When he was eventually successful he slid the contents out on the table. They were photos. Photos of Archie, Nicky, Johnny, the others all laying dead in the gallery. Sean's eyes grew wide as he took in the photos. "What the hell is this?" he asked in a voice of disbelief.

"That's what we want to know," Detective Willams responded, "Now start talking." Sean stared at the photos now spread out before him. "Playing along always makes it easier, Sean. Especially easier to protect you from your Italian friends. You and I both know that they'll be looking for retribution," Detective Doyle said, leaning in to try to capture eye contact with Sean.

Sean barely heard his words. He was intently studying the photos. Finally, after studying the pictures for a full minute or more he looked up at Detective Doyle, "Where's Sonny, Louie, and the kid?"

36

The square, central quad was surrounded by regal stone buildings on three sides. Canopied by tall, aged trees flush with green foliage in the summer, the absence of leaves already on some of the trees revealed the gray clouds that filled the sky. Drizzle and wind accompanied unusually cool temperatures, driving the normal bustlers of the institution indoors for comfort with late sleep, movies, and books.

Even the modern looking building on the far end of the square lost some of its contrasting impact, but still faithfully represented the College's push to ensure connection with modern times and the modern student. The Berkshire College Art School was housed inside the modern building. The exterior of the rectangular main section of the building featured large maple wooden panels for the top two floors above the first floor window walls, giving a clear view of the school's lobby and gallery. The far end of the main building transitioned to a section that was clad in bright silver metal, taller than the rest of the building. Upon his arrival on campus, Louie thought that it resembled the bow of a mighty ship.

He had survived the debacle at the gallery, and barely managed to grab the jade bixie before escaping Sonny's pursuit. He entered the art school through the main doors, walked through the lobby and past the gallery entrance, and made his way up the one flight of stairs to the second floor. After exiting the stairwell and rounding the corner he made his way to office 210. He knocked on the door and waited impatiently, hugging the bixie to his chest under his jacket.

Almost immediately, Chad Longfellow answered the door. Being a weekend, he was not dressed in his normal professor attire, choosing instead chinos and a Berkshire College sweatshirt with the collar of a blue polo shirt peeking out of the neck. Chad inspected Louie for a second before speaking. Louie looked haggard to Chad, obviously lacking sleep, fresh clothes and a shower. Chad didn't care. "About time," he started curtly, "get in here and tell me what happened."

"It was a disaster," Louie started, "an absolute disaster." He sat in the guest chair next to Chad's desk and pulled out the bixie that was wrapped in a small towel. Unwrapping the towel, he placed the jade statuette on Chad's desk. "I did manage to grab this while I was escaping. At least it's something, I guess," Louie continued, shifting his attention to Chad to see his reaction.

"You guess? You guess?!" Chad responded, beginning to lose the battle with his anger. He resettled himself. "Tell me exactly what happened and how it got so screwed up. I want to understand exactly what went wrong and where we stand."

"We had it all set up just like we planned. I helped you find the place. We amazingly got the alarm system under our control, and the girls trusted it. I worked Johnny, and he talked Sonny into doing the job. I even got them to agree on using you, well 'my guy', as a fence. Things were all set up," Louie explained.

"So how, exactly, did it all go so bad?" Chad asked, leveling his voice to emphasize the main focus of his inquiry.

"I'm not sure," Louie lied, "I've been trying to work that out. All that I can figure is that one of the senior guys found out and showed up to put a stop to it." What Louie had actually concluded on the trip to Connecticut was how badly he screwed up by telling Archie and Dominic about the planned robbery. He had let his anger over how Sonny treated him get the better of him, leading to the poor decision of telling the senior gangsters. While it wasn't the first time Louie had let his anger get the best of his decision making, he had never expected the slaughter that ensued. What he had expected was for them to intervene with Sonny, penalizing him by taking a larger cut from the job, hoping that was enough to make the job financially worthless for him.

"So, we show up at the gallery, disable the security system and things are going along fine. All of a sudden these other gangsters show up shooting. It was like a war zone, Chad, I'm telling you, I was lucky to escape with my life...and this statue thing, we can sell that at least, right?"

Chad was not yet done with his inquisition. "When I called you about the idea for this robbery you said that you could handle it. All of the time we spent developing the plan. Me driving down to Westchester County to meet with you because you couldn't be 'away that long' as you put it. Me working with those girls and pretending to be interested in that gullible ditz Meya. Me kissing asses, hobnobbing with those idiots in charge of the College art shows just so I could get the position in charge of obtaining the pieces. Then risking my entire reputation by scamming both the artists and the college so that we could get the pieces that I wanted in that gallery, the pieces that would bring good money on the black market. You're telling me that one jade statue is going to make up for all of that?!" Chad's nose was now positioned about an inch from Louie's face as his tirade grew in crescendo the longer he spoke.

"Well what about insurance? Any way we can get some money from that?" Louie asked, "I need something out of this. I have to restart again, I can't go back."

"No! There is no insurance money for you!" Chad responded, "Insurance pays the artists for the pieces that are destroyed, and the remaining pieces will be returned after they're released and thoroughly cleaned. I'm sure that the College will face several lawsuits on this, and no doubt all of the heat will be directed at me. Of course, there's no way I'm going down without taking you out as well. That's why I had you pick up and deliver the art to the gallery. I made sure that you ended up on the cameras and the key card you used to access the storage area wasn't mine, but one that was reported stolen by another professor. I can read the headlines now 'Mobster Familiar With Berkshire College Robs School to Stage Art Heist'. I of course will be happy to tell them all about you, how you staged yourself as an employee of the school, and how I found you out and banished you. That's all that I need and I walk away. You don't."

Louie boiled at this response and lunged at Chad who deflected his attack pushing Louie off balance and to the back of the office. Chad quickly threw his office door open just in time to see two students walking in the hall on their way to do some weekend work.

"Everything ok, professor?" one of the students asked.

"Why yes, of course, why wouldn't it be?" Chad replied, smiling at the students and calming his breathing as best he could. After they passed, he stood in the doorway being sure not to leave himself susceptible to another attack from Louie. Chad then turned to face Louie contemplating his next move.

Chad quickly reached and grabbed the bixie. "I'll be seeing after this. You're right, maybe I can salvage something out of selling this," he stated.

"You can salvage, what about me?" Louie asked.

"You, no, you get nothing," Chad seethed in a whispered voice to avoid the attention of any other students that may be in the hallway. "Besides, it's going to take me a while to find someone who is even interested in this, and move it quickly before administration or the police come asking questions," he continued, "but you? You, Louie, and I are done. Move on."

Louie could feel the rage rising again inside himself. It took all of his strength to resist the temptation to attack the Professor again. Louie didn't trust himself or how far he might take things with the stress and trauma of the recent events weighing on him like lead. As he stepped past Chad to leave he paused, staring menacingly into the man's eyes. "We might be done here now, but we are far from done." At this he stepped out and left.

Chad breathed a sigh of relief at Louie's departure, re-entering his office and locking the door. He studied the bixie statuette, turning it around in his hands. '*You had better be worth something, my little friend*', he thought to himself. After turning the piece over in his hands a few times, he reached for the black lock box that he kept under his desk. Unlocking the box with the key held on a chain around his neck, he first removed the box contents, a limited edition of Jane Eyre that Meya had given him for Christmas and a 9mm pistol that he kept in case things went awry with the robbery, which they had. Deciding quickly on priorities, he put the book on a shelf, the pistol in his waistband, and the bixie statuette in the lock box.

"Ok, time to make some calls and find a buyer," he said aloud. '*This is going to take a while especially if I have to find someone overseas.*' He then opened his laptop and started to investigate potential buyers, thinking '*this better be worth the cost.*'

37

"Sonny is at my mom's," was all that Jake could muster.

Sarah looked at him with terror in her eyes, covering her mouth as she gasped. "But how? How could he find us?"

"I don't know," Jake responded, still bewildered, "I didn't tell anyone but you that I was from Vermont. Did you say something to him?"

"No, I don't even know Sonny," she replied, the worry still evident in her features.

They both took time to consider what was happening and how it happened. "Didn't you tell Deniz when you interviewed at The Athena?" she asked.

"No, I don't think so," Jake said, straining to remember, "even if I had I wouldn't have told him Pine Grove."

"Well, they know your last name. It would be an easy enough internet search to find you," Sarah added.

After a pause Jake suddenly remembered, "I think I told Zehab the night that he tried the moussaka."

"That's right, you did," Sarah agreed, "I would have thought that he was too drunk to remember."

"Well, he must have, because I don't know anyone else who knows Sonny and his crew and would have told them. No one else but you knew," Jake concluded. "It doesn't really matter how he knows, the fact is he's here now. We have to get to my mother's. C'mon let's go."

They hurried to the truck and sped to Jake's childhood home. When they arrived Jake told Sarah to stay in the truck. He gave her the cellphone and told her to call the police if he wasn't out soon.

"No way! I'm not staying in the truck. We are in this together, Jake, remember?" Sarah argued.

"I know, and we are, but it's not safe Sarah," he argued back.

It didn't take long before it was decided. Jake and Sarah walked to the front door and knocked.

Jake's mother, Mary, opened the door slowly. She had tears in her eyes and was evidently shaken by the events of the day. "Mom, are you ok?" Jake immediately blurted out, starting to move to hug her. Jake stopped as soon as he saw Sonny's silhouette behind his mother and the gun stuck into her side.

"She's just fine Jake. And you brought your squeeze as well, how wonderful. Why don't you both come in nice and slowly so that we can talk?" Sonny's tone established control of the situation.

Once inside Sonny ordered them to sit on the couch while he stood behind Jake's mother, who sat at the table in the connected kitchen. "So, Jake," Sonny started without delay, "you and Louie thought you could pull the double-cross and get away with it, huh?"

Jake looked confused; Sarah looked worried. Mustering some courage, Jake responded, "Double-cross? I have no idea what you're talking about. And I'm not answering another question until you let her go."

Sonny simply chuckled in disbelief and then leveled his gaze on Jake, responding in a very serious tone, "I don't think you understand how this works. You answer all of my questions or your mother dies." The seriousness of Sonny's words hung in the air ominously, leaving no doubt of his intention or willingness to carry it out.

"Now, let me try again. You two thought you would get away with this?" Sonny continued.

"I have no idea what double-cross you're talking about," Jake responded.

Sonny roared back at Jake, his face instantly crimson and the veins in his neck protruding in rage, "You rub out my entire crew and ruin my family, and now you have the balls to deny it! And all for some freakin' Chinese statue, or whatever. I should blow her brains all over the place, and then your little girlfriend's next!" Sonny slammed the barrel of the gun into the side of Mary's head. She started sobbing instantly, muttering a prayer quietly to herself.

"Wait Sonny, I swear I don't know what you're talking about," Jake pleaded, panicked. "I went to the job just like you told me to. I sat in the van and waited until I heard shooting. Then I went in to try to help and everyone was dead. Well, everyone except Nicky, but he was shot and dying quickly. I couldn't help him."

"Nicky was alive when I left him. He would have contacted me," Sonny responded, still enraged but no longer yelling. "You're still lying, Jake. That's it," he said, cocking the pistol and again jamming it into Mary's head.

"You're right, I am," Jake responded, holding his hands up and towards Sonny in a physical act of admittance, "I shot Nicky, but he was going to shoot me. That's the truth, I promise. After that I took off, I got Sarah, and headed north. That's the truth Sonny, you have to believe me."

"I don't have to believe anything," Sonny responded, "I have the gun. And you're still not telling me about working with Louie."

"I didn't work with Louie, honest. Sonny, I don't know anything about that," Jake replied.

"Louie was in the gallery, but he didn't get shot. He knew what was coming. He ran out of the gallery carrying a statue. Some bixie," Sonny further explained.

"Sonny, if I was in on it, why would I run into the building when the shooting started?" Jake asked.

This caused Sonny to pause and consider the validity of Jake's point. After a second he moved the gun from Mary's head, but still stayed put behind her. Mary sobbed a little louder, but her muscles relaxed slightly. The cadence of her soft prayer also shifted with the slightest hint of relief.

"Ok, so if you weren't working with Louie, then where is he?" Sonny asked in a more normal tone, the amber color draining some from his face and his veins restored to their natural condition.

"I don't know, honest," Jake responded.

"Well, we still have a problem. See, I think that you do know, and I need that statue back," Sonny explained.

"I don't know Sonny, I'm telling you," Jake again pleaded.

"I don't believe you," Sonny replied, more in control at this point, "and I think that you need some more motivation to remember." He again stuck the barrel of the gun against Mary's head, this time not as violently but with clear intent. "Think hard, Jake, you sure you don't remember?"

"I don't, Sonny, please stop. I don't know," Jake pleaded even more intensely. His mother looked at him with terror in her eyes. Jake felt helpless.

"Stop!" Sarah exclaimed suddenly. All three of them turned to look at her. "I know where Louie is," she declared.

"How?" Jake asked, with a tone of complete surprise.

"Because Louie is my brother."

*　　　　*　　　　*

Jake hadn't said a word to Sarah since her big revelation. After driving in silence for a while, Sarah decided to break the ice. "Jake, I'm sorry. I couldn't tell you about Louie and me, and I didn't know that it would lead to this." Jake continued driving in silence, not even acknowledging Sarah's words. Sarah reached out and touched Jake's arm. "I guess that it's time that you know the whole truth about me, and Louie."

Sarah continued, anticipating no response from Jake. "I told you about my ex-boyfriend. How he threatened me, how he hit me," her voice trailing off slightly, "well as I lay on the floor, my face on fire from his punch, blood on my shirt and the carpet, I ran into the closest room which was the bathroom. I locked the door, but knew that he could break that down effortlessly and the window was too small for even me to climb out. I fortunately was able to call my brother to come help me. I know that he has a temper but I had no choice." Jake kept his gaze intently on the road, but his attention was fully focused on Sarah's words.

"In a few minutes I heard Louie's truck come tearing into the driveway. He stormed in the front door and confronted my ex. I heard the yelling followed by loud crashes. Then there was nothing but silence. After a minute or so I unlocked the door and ventured into the living room only to see Louie kneeling over the dead body. Louie killed him, Jake, he killed him to protect *me*."

Jake lowered his gaze for the first time on the drive, "I'm sorry, Sarah, I didn't know, but…"

"Wait, there's more for you to hear," Sarah interrupted. "My ex's family is very powerful back home. They own car dealerships and other businesses. They weren't about to let the murder of their only son go unpunished, even if he beat me." Jake sat in silence again, listening. "We had to run Jake. I don't just mean head to the city, I mean run. Louie and I have been all over from Maryland into Connecticut. I told you that. When we were in Connecticut, Louie got a job at the Art School at Berkshire College working in the stock room and stuff."

"Well, a professor there befriended Louie. Took him to the bar one night. After enough drinks, Louie tells him what happened. The professor threatened to tell the police unless Louie helped him steal some paintings. Louie told me this after he got home, and there was no doubt in my mind that he would do it and was getting set up, so I left without even looking back. Looking back just gets you in trouble. Louie followed my cue and we headed to the city without a word. We managed to get a place."

"So Louie's your roommate?" Jake asked just to confirm what he was confident that he already knew.

"Yes," replied Sarah, "that's why you couldn't come to my place and meet him."

"And that explains the strange look between you two when he came into the restaurant looking for me," Jake further confirmed.

"Yes," Sarah again replied. "Louie did some petty crime to get us some money and got noticed by the Mafia guys. I hated that he got hooked up with them, but the money was good and, as you know, it isn't inexpensive to live in New York."

"So did you know about the robbery?" Jake asked.

"No, that was all Louie. He was trying to make one big score so that we could head overseas. Even though it seemed like we had finally outrun my ex's family, Louie wanted to put as much distance between them and us."

Jake processed this for a few more miles. He then turned to look at Sarah for the first time on the trip. "I believe you, Sarah. I still want to put all of that behind us, if you still do too."

Sarah's eyes teared up as she replied. "Of course I do, Jake, I want us more than you'll ever know." Jake reached his hand down to hers.

"You think that Louie is with this Professor?" Jake asked.

"I do," she replied, "but I can call him and find out if you give me the burner."

Jake reached into his pocket, took out his phone, and handed it to Sarah. She dialed and waited, "Hey, it's me. Are you ok?...good...are you with that Professor, what was his name...yeah, Chad, are you with him?...well it gets worse, Sonny has taken Jake's mother hostage, and he says that you took a statue from that robbery?...we have to get it back ...yes, I have no doubt that he will kill her, and we only have 24 hours to get it back, do you have it?" Sarah's face fell, "can you get it?...ok, I'm sorry, but we have to get it back, we can't let her die...we're about an hour away...ok, I'll see you soon. Be careful." Sarah hung up.

"Ok, he doesn't have it, but he's going to go and get it back," Sarah said trying to reassure Jake, but Jake could see the worry in her eyes.

38

Louie had every intention to return, anyway. '*There's no way that prick is taking the only thing salvageable from this mess*', Louie thought as soon as he left the professor and calmed down some. Now as he sat outside the art building, having just spoken to Sarah, the weight of endangering the life of Jake's mother further motivated him. Things had quickly gotten out of hand, again. And it was again fallout from his temper, first with Sarah's ex and then trying to set Sonny up for a fall with Archie and Dominic. He had to at least try to fix things this time, especially with someone completely innocent involved.

He sat on a bench outside the art school, his attention solely focused on the third window in from the end of the building on the second floor. It was the office of Dr. Chad Longfellow, and was the only lighted office at the late hour. As Louie breathed in his hands to warm them, the light in the office finally extinguished. At this he got up and stood behind a shrub that allowed him to watch the front door inconspicuously. In only a few minutes Louie watched Chad leave the art school.

Waiting a few minutes to ensure that Chad didn't return and that there wasn't any other activity, Louie made his way to the front door. While the building was open during the day, the glass doors were locked at night. Before he searched for an alternate entrance or was forced into breaking and entering, Louie pulled the key card from his pocket. This was the same key card that Chad had given him to gain access to the loading dock to take the art to View gallery in the city. While

Chad had told him that the key card had been reported stolen, Louie knew that action was often slow or forgotten at large institutions like the College. He took a chance and passed the key card across the reader next to the main entrance doors. An immediate click was heard, and Louie opened the door. He held the door open while he hid the key card behind a nearby brick. *'They'll need this to get in'*, he thought.

He made his way to office 210. The office door was also locked, and he knew his key card wouldn't work to open it. Prepared, he pulled a notched piece of plastic that he had cut from an empty bottle of Coke from his pocket and leaned his body gently against the door to push it into the jamb. Feathering in the piece of plastic, in a matter of seconds he had worked the latch free. *'Fancy key card security, and it still only took me a few seconds to get in'*, he thought, shaking his head.

Louie looked around the professor's office. There were shelves of books on art from different eras, essays on a variety of topics ranging from the French Renaissance to counterculture and race relations. There were a few small art pieces on the shelves, and numerous posters and pictures on all of the available wall space. 'Galerie Maeght, Andre Derain' Louie read on one poster with a sketched figure of a round, nude woman. *'Whatever that is'*, he thought, shifting his attention back to the business of finding the bixie. He looked around the office, but found no sign of the statuette. When he discovered the black lock box he figured that it had to be inside.

As he began to work on the box his cell phone rang. It was Sarah. "Sarah?...good...yeah, I'm already inside his office. I think that I found it...Room 210 in the art school. I left the key card behind the brick near the door...yeah, see you soon."

He hung up and focused on the box. He considered trying to pick the lock, but didn't have his tools. He also considered heading to a studio to look for some but that would take too long. Louie decided to go with a more basic approach and smashed the corner of the lid on the edge of the desk. The corner of the lid bent back slightly. To Louie's relief, the bixie only thudded inside the box, and he could feel foam padding on the inside of the box offering some protection for the statuette from Louie's chosen method of extracting it. After a few more impacts the lid deformed sufficiently, allowing Louie to unlatch the lid and remove the bixie, still intact. '*Good thing it's stone*', Louie thought while setting the box on Chad's desk and examining the statuette.

He was fascinated by the small but powerful fantastical figure. He studied the contours of the stone, running his fingernail along the imperfections of the natural jade. He wondered about the age of the piece, the meaning behind it, and what normally came to his mind first, the amount that he could sell it for. He blew the small amount of dust from the figure with his breath, pausing to look into the face of the small beast. As he stared at it he knew that he wasn't going to sell it, he wasn't going to capitalize on it to get money to fund he and Sarah's next move. He knew that he was going to hand it to Jake and tell him to go and free his mother. And then he and maybe Sarah would start again in a new place. '*Maybe it's time to try the West coast*', he thought.

"You just don't learn, do you?" came the voice from behind him. Chad stood in the office doorway pointing his gun at Louie. Louie broke his stare at the statuette and shifted focus to Chad. Chad's features were fixed on him, "I actually hoped that you would have been smart enough just to stay away, but knew that you were too stupid and stubborn to do that."

Louie tried to quickly think of a way out of the situation but didn't come up with one. He considered throwing the bixie at Chad but knew that would be futile in the confines of the small office. Before he could decide on any action Chad spoke again, "This ends now, but not in my office. Too hard to cover that up. C'mon, move." Chad gestured with the gun, backing out of the doorway to allow Louie to move in front of him. Louie looked as best he could around the hall for any other signs of life, but saw no one else in the building. "Downstairs to the gallery," Chad commanded. Concealing the gun close to his body, he and Louie made their way down the stairs.

They entered the art school lobby. It was a sparse, industrial space with a few dark leather couches and chairs on a deep pile light gray rug cut in a shape that resembled an amoeba to Louie. There was a coffee table made from the trunk of a large tree in the center of the rug. A directory for Berkshire College, a notice for an upcoming student art show, and a striking piece of art sat on the table. A placard located near the piece stated that it was made by dropping molten metal onto ice resulting in splashed, jagged shapes that were built upon with each subsequent layer, some of which were bent to capture the artist's vision. The effect of the final piece was to portray a metallic flower that was too threatening and sharp to touch.

As they began to cross the lobby to the gallery both Chad and Louie were startled by banging on the exterior doors. Sarah was hammering on the door with her palms, while Jake scrambled to find the key card. Louie capitalized the distraction and lunged at Chad who fired reactionarily, missing Louie by millimeters. Louie wrapped his arms around Chad's waist driving him over the back of the couch, both men tumbling to the floor. Louie lost control of the bixie which rolled across the large rug stopping beside one of the chairs. Chad held fast to the gun, but caught his leg on the metal piece of art on the coffee table as they tumbled, gashing his left thigh, and causing him to cry out in pain.

As this played out, Jake and Sarah burst into the lobby. Jake started to move forward to help but was rebuffed by Louie shouting, "No! I got this. Get the statue and get out of here. Get this back to your mom." Sarah reached for the bixie as Chad and Louie continued their struggle.

Retrieving the piece, Jake and Sarah tried to run to the doors to leave, but they were now blocked as Chad and Louie crashed down in their path as they struggled. Jake saw the panic in Sarah's eyes. "C'mon, we'll find another way out," Jake said commandingly, taking Sarah's hand and heading down the main corridor to look for an emergency exit.

As they ran from the men they heard another gunshot, and stopped to look back to see who the victim might be. "Run, Jen, run, and don't look back!" Louie called out, he and Chad still fighting for control of the weapon.

Jake and Sarah bolted down the hall seeing the bright red 'EXIT' sign at the other end of the long hallway. "There, we need to go there," Jake yelled, pulling Sarah along.

The next shot echoed through the long hallway. Instinctively they paused again, hoping to see Louie run around the corner. They stepped into the doorway of a large art studio classroom to stay out of sight, listening.

The voice echoed towards them, but it wasn't Louie's. It filled the space with the ominous news, "Your brothers dead." Sarah shuddered, her eyes widening and tears forming instantly at the news. But Chad wasn't done yet, "And I'm coming for you next."

39

"C'mon we gotta move," Jake said quietly but urgently, pulling Sarah along with him. Sarah, still stunned at the news of her brother's death, absently allowed Jake to pull her along. The couple moved deeper into the studio they had entered. It had a section of long tables next to an area of easels positioned in a circle around a center stool with a display of plastic fruit. There were palettes and brushes on the stool at each easel. *'No weapons here'*, thought Jake.

They made their way through the door that connected the first studio with a second. This studio contained tables similar to the previous studio, but each supported a papier mâché sculpture of the human form on wire frames, each completed to different extents. While the sculptures were several feet tall, Jake again surmised that the wireframe figures would not make good weapons.

His concentration was broken by Chad's voice again echoing through the school. "I'm coming, and there's nowhere to hide," he bellowed.

At the conclusion of Chad's latest threat Jake observed a new light shine through the studio windows. "He's turning on the lights in the studios," Jake surmised out loud. "Sarah, we need to keep moving. We need to weave our way through the studios to the exit before he finds us," he pleaded with Sarah, who was still in shock.

Jake stopped and focused on Sarah, gripping her shoulders and moving his face close to hers. He spoke softly but firmly, looking her in the eye, trying to garner a similar response from her. "Sarah, I know that it's hard, but we have to go.

Please Sarah…or is it Jen?" Sarah broke from her fog at Jake's use of the name, 'Jen'. Not waiting for her response, Jake asked, "Sarah, who is Jen?'

After a pause Sarah responded, "Jen is my given name."

Jake tried to take in this information quickly, but struggled to understand. Sarah continued, "My name is Jen, but after what happened back home I've had to change it many times. You met me as Sarah, and honestly Jake, that is the person that I want to be. That's the person that you know."

The light from another studio across the hall from the first shown through the windows to the hallway. Chad continued his menacing blustering, "Come out, come out wherever you are."

"Sarah, we can't let Louie die in vain. We have to move and get out of here." Sarah nodded and ran with Jake to the next studio, only two away from the building's emergency exit. They pushed through the door with 'Hot Shop' printed on the wire reinforced window. This gallery was laid out differently than the others. There were three industrial tables in the middle of the large room. On one wall there were three furnaces that lined up with each table. A steel shroud ran the length of the wall above the furnaces, with signs labeling each furnace as Glory Hole 1 through 3. There were also various tools at each station ranging from hand tools set out on the benches, buckets holding several other long handled hand tools, and long metallic hollow blow pipes standing in rings welded to the corner of each workstation.

"I think we're in a glass studio," Sarah said.

They moved through the dark workshop, both turning when they saw a new light come on from across the hallway. 'He'll be heading to this side of the hallway next," Jake surmised, "we have to hurry. Go!" They bumped past a few shelves, making their way into the main studio when they heard the crash behind them. A glass piece had fallen as they rushed by in their haste.

"Ahhh, my prey has revealed itself," yelled Chad from the hallway.

Jake and Sarah knew that Chad was now headed directly to them. "We have to hide," Jake urged, "quick, back here." They ducked into a storage area the length of the wall opposite the furnaces. This area contained more tools as well as round storage bins on the wall containing glass rods of different sizes and containers of glass powdered frit. Jake and Sarah hid behind some storage bins and waited, trying not to make any more noise.

The light in the main studio space came on almost immediately. They could hear Chad enter the studio. "Aww what a shame, this piece is broken," Chad said, his voice taking on a more maniacal tone with each sentence, 'Tsk, tsk, tsk, you two weren't very careful." In an instant, a sudden cascade of breaking glass encased the room, causing both Jake and Sarah to jump, startled.

Jake started to step out of their hiding place to try to get a line of sight on Chad. "Jake, don't," Sarah whispered in a pleading tone, grabbed him. Jake looked back at her, removed her hand from his arm, and then kept moving slowly until he could see his pursuer.

Chad had knocked the entire shelf over in an act of rage. 'He's completely lost it', Jake thought, immediately regretting the decision to hide in the storage space with only one way out. Chad started to make his way into the main gallery. "Olly olly oxen free," he yelled with a high pitch tone that caused Sarah to shudder. "You're never going to make it out of here alive," he continued, singing the words with a whimsical musical melody for effect.

Sarah reached out to Jake to prompt him to return to their hiding place, but Jake was focused on Chad. He noticed that Chad was walking with a limp, and that there was blood on his left pant leg. *'He's hurt'*, he thought.

Jake stepped back and knelt with Sarah once more. His instructions to her were brief, but she nodded, understanding. As they heard Chad pounding on one of the workstations with something metallic, laughing maniacally as loud as he could, Jake rose and walked to the entrance of the storage unit. He called out to Chad, "Hey, over here!" Chad, who was holding the gun in one hand and a long blow tube in the other turned to look at Jake.

"Well, well, well, what do we have here?" Chad asked, raising the pistol.

"I wouldn't do that," Jake offered.

"And why is that?" Chad asked, intentionally cocking his head in mock inquisitiveness.

"Because, you'll never get the statue back," Jake replied.

Chad started to laugh maniacally again. "I don't care about that statue anymore." Chad leveled his voice and squared his gaze on Jake as he continued, "See, my focus now is to make sure I don't leave any witnesses."

"Well, that isn't going to happen," Jake responded as calmly as he could muster.

"I think that decision is up to the person with the *gun!*" Chad yelled.

"I don't think so," Jake countered, "see, as we were talking, Sarah was leaving. We split up when we heard you looking for us." Jake let this statement sink in for a second before continuing. "*She* is a witness, and now she's gone, and I'm the only person here that knows where she is."

Chad considered this for a second while he held his aim on Jake. As his face revealed that he had finished his internal calculations and come to a conclusion, he again leveled his gaze at Jake. "That's bullshit," he said dryly and evenly. "That little girl would never leave your side, not after I killed her brother like that. See, as I see it, you're bluffing." Jake shifted his weight and breathed in a quick breath. "And there's the tell," Chad concluded.

Jake immediately ducked back into the storage area, as Chad fired a shot in his direction. "Come'ere!" Chad yelled as he limped to the edge of the storage area. He positioned himself at the entrance, being careful not to get too close and expose himself to attack. The storage area was dark, and he couldn't see Jake or Sarah. Using the blow tube that he still held he flipped the light switch near the entrance to the storage unit. As the light came on Sarah swung the container of glass powder, showering the powdered shards into Chad's face blinding him instantly. Jake immediately pushed past her, landing a heavy metal bar squarely on Chad's head, knocking him to the floor. As he hit the ground he dropped both the blow tube and the pistol.

Chad laid motionless on the floor. Jake and Sarah stood over Chad for only a second to make sure he wasn't moving. Jake then bent and pressed his fingers to Chad's neck. "He still has a pulse." Suddenly they could hear sirens in the distance. "We have to go!" Jake exclaimed, taking Sarah's hand and trying to lead her out of the gallery.

After only a few steps, Sarah let go. "Wait, I have to get it," she said.

"Just leave the gun," Jake responded, the urgency evident in his voice.

"Not the gun," Sarah replied, returning quickly with the bixie. She could see the realization in Jake's eyes.

"Jesus, we almost left without it."

"It's ok, we got it. Let's go."

40

The rain pounded on the windshield of the Ford pickup as Jake and Sarah sped back to Vermont. Sarah had fallen asleep in the passenger seat. She was curled up with her feet underneath her, the hood of her sweatshirt pulled over her head as she leaned against Jake's side. Jake looked down at her, noticing the gentle way that strands of her hair escaped the confines of her hood. He thought back to their time together.

He recalled the attraction that he had for her when they first met at the restaurant. He smiled recalling their time talking and cooking in the kitchen of The Athena, and their walks along the river. He could feel her arms around his waist and the form of her being on his back as she clung to him on his motorcycle. A warmth filled his body as he came to realize how she had been beside him the entire time, even following the botched robbery. *'She knows how to run and she didn't'*, he thought. *'She stayed.'*

Jake drove on for several more miles, feeling Sarah's warmth on his side, before his eyelids started to droop significantly. At one point he caught himself asleep, jarring himself awake with realization. This awoke Sarah as well.

Rubbing sleep from her eyes, Sarah asked, "Are you ok? Where are we?"

"Still about two hours out," replied Jake. "I need you to help keep me awake, if you can," he requested.

"Ok, sure, how about some music?" Sarah asked, tuning the radio and finding an all night country music station. The DJ announced that it was overnight classics while the music from the next song started. "Oh, I love this song," Sarah said, turning the volume up slightly, "I haven't heard it in years, since I was in West Virginia actually." She concentrated on the beginning of the song. "This is Kathy Mattea, *Love at the Five & Dime.*"

The young couple rode on in the rain listening to the steel guitar and Kathy singing the simple lyrics about another young couple. Jake heard Sarah singing along softly. As the song ended Jake interjected, "Sarah, I'm so sorry about your past. You deserve better than that. I never knew you as Jen, but I think that you should be yourself. If that is Jen, then I love Jen. If that is Sarah, then I love Sarah. I just know that I love you no matter what, just like I know that you love me."

She wrapped her arms around him and snuggled closely. "I love you too, Jake, no matter what. And Sarah is just fine."

As they got closer to Pine Grove they had to stop for fuel. Jake pulled into the Champlain Farms gas station. "I'm going to get some coffee, do you want anything?" Jake asked.

"No, I'm good," she replied. Jake jumped out with his wallet, started the pump, and walked inside. Returning to the cab, they started again towards his mother's house.

"I used your phone and called Sonny and told him that we're on our way," Sarah said.

"Why?" Jake asked. "We lost any chance of surprising him."

"Exactly," replied Sarah, "we don't want to surprise him or have him think that we aren't coming or anything like that. If I wasn't so tired I would have been thinking clearly and called him earlier in the trip."

"Yeah, I guess that makes sense," Jake concluded, "thanks."

Jake started driving again with a renewed sense of urgency and purpose as they entered Pine Grove. Whether the caffeine, adrenaline, or both, Jake sped around the town green and past The Blue Heron without even a notice. Both arms were nearly rigid as he steered, his left leg twitching like a piston in the engine of a performance race car. Sarah was now sitting quietly in the passenger seat. She also kept her eyes fixed on the road, her hands clenched together tightly, one thumb rubbing over the other.

As they got close to Jake's mother's house Jake finally spoke, "You ready?"

"I am," replied Sarah evenly.

"Ok, let's finally end this," Jake declared as he pulled into the small driveway on the side of the house knowing that this offered a difficult viewing angle from the house. Jake leapt from the truck almost before it had come to a complete stop. Sarah watched as he quickly made his way to the small shed in the backyard. She kept watch on the side door of the house while Jake was inside the shed. Even though he was only inside for a few seconds, she held her breath the entire time. Jake emerged carrying his father's shotgun, concealing it along the side of his body opposite the house, and made his way back to the truck. Sarah had climbed out to meet him, carrying the bixie.

Jake bent slightly and made his way to the side door of the house. He turned the knob slowly, confirming that it was unlocked. He removed his hand and nodded at Sarah who replaced his hand with hers on the knob. She turned the knob slowly and pushed the door open while Jake lowered the gun and started inside. He immediately saw his mother seated in a kitchen chair across the room. Her arms appeared to be tied behind her back. Even though her mouth was gagged she was desperately trying to communicate with Jake through a flurry of grunts, repeatedly dashing her eyes to her left. Jake instinctively took another step into the room.

"Nice try kid," Sonny said as he leveled the pistol into the side of Jake's head, "but this ain't my first rodeo." Sonny reached his left hand and took the gun from Jake's hands. "Now, why don't you and your little girl join us properly." Sonny stepped back allowing Jake and Sarah to enter the room. He closed the door while giving his instructions, "Over there, by your mother."

Jake bent to reassure his mother. "No, no. That ain't happening. You had your chance to keep this civil until you walked through the door with the gun," Sonny intervened, pointing the gun at each of them for emphasis. "You," he said pointing the barrel at Sarah, "take a seat next to Mom."

"We have what you want," Sarah said before moving to pull over another chair. She pulled the bixie from her sweatshirt holding it up for Sonny to see.

"See, now that would have been a smarter way to start this thing, Jake. But you had to go and piss me off with the macho shit," Sonny said to Jake, shaking his head. "Put it on the table," he continued. Sarah did as instructed. Sonny reached over and picked up the bixie. "This is it? This little dragon thing? All of this trouble for some freakin' paper weight?!" Sonny's features were turning hard, his jaw clenched as tightly as he gripped the pistol. "I cannot fucking believe this," he growled.

Seeing Sonny's growing rage, Sarah intervened again, "Ok, I'm sitting down, just like you told me to." She pulled over a chair and sat, hoping that her compliance would help reestablish a sense of control for Sonny.

"Take the duct tape and tape her to the chair," Sonny directed Jake. Jake took the duct tape from the table and did as directed. He then stood and looked at Sonny, whose face was still a shade of crimson. Sonny stood quietly, staring intently at Jake for a full minute. Jake was sweating, unsure of his next move. "You know, I was just going to do you Jake. Let the civilians live with the threat of death if they said anything to anyone. But since you entered my existence I've lost everything...over a statue. No, not gonna end that way. I've had to pay, so you will too."

Jake's eyes widened at this statement. His breathing was shallow and quick, not knowing what Sonny had planned.

"There will be no witnesses," Sonny threatened coldly.

Sonny swung the gun towards Mary quickly taking aim and cocking the hammer of the gun. Jake leapt to protect his mother as the shot rang out. He felt the hard floor under his shoulder as he pushed his mother backwards to the floor, shifting Sarah as well in the process. Jake waited for the pain to shoot through him. The fact that a shot from that close would instantly kill him had not even entered his mind. He only thought of saving his mother and Sarah.

However, as the sound of the shot rang down, Jake realized that he didn't feel shot. '*And I'm still breathing*', he thought.

Quickly checking, he didn't see any blood on his body. He turned his head to assess Sonny's next move, but Sonny was laying on the floor on his back. There Jake saw the pool of blood that he expected to find under himself.

Unsure of what happened, he frantically looked around the room for answers. His mother was crying but still alive, as was Sarah who was beginning to lift her head. There was no blood on either of them. He continued scanning until he stopped on the picture window. There, through the window, he saw Red standing on the deck still holding up his pistol, a single small hole in the clear glass.

Derek suddenly burst into the kitchen, and quickly surveyed the situation. "Is everyone ok?" he asked, not waiting for an answer as he made his way to help Mary and Sarah out of their restraints.

Confirming that the women were being cared for, Jake walked outside and met Red in the driveway. "Red...how?" was the only inquiry that his mind could manage.

"Sarah," Red replied simply, "she called me when you stopped for gas. I knew something was wrong when that guy came to visit me, but I couldn't piece it together. She filled me in quickly. I called Derek to come get me. Looks like it was just in time."

Jake fought back his tears. "You're the savior again, Red."

"I might have fired the shot, but don't sell yourself short, Jake," Red interrupted, looking Jake squarely in the eyes, "you jumped in front of them. You were willing to sacrifice your life for theirs. That is being the hero, Jake."

The two men were interrupted by Sarah running out of the house. She ran to Jake and wrapped her arms around his waist. "Please tell me it's over...please," she pleaded into his chest.

"It is, Sarah, it is."

41

Silvio sat alone in the back of the delicatessen. The weight of the betrayal still consumed him. He stared blankly into space, the fingers of his right hand tapping lightly on the glass of vino he was actively ignoring. A knock on the door leading to the front of the delicatessen broke Silvio's concentration. "Yes?" he called out.

A delicatessen employee opened the door and leaned in, "Sorry to disturb you Mr. Amoretti, there are two detectives here to see you."

Silvio's instincts kicked in as he straightened some in his chair and adjusted his tie. Even his tone hardened as he replied, "Yeah, make them wait a few minutes then send them in."

After a minute or two the door was opened by the same employee, and the two detectives walked in. Silvio recognized the taller, dark skinned detective as Detective Duante Williams. He did not know the name of the other detective. This bothered Silvio. *'I used to know all of these guys back in the day. What's happened to me?'*, he thought without changing his demeanor.

"Mr. Amoretti, I'm Detective Doyle and this is Detective Williams," the shorter detective started. Silvio sat motionless and silent. "We wanted to ask you a few questions about the situation at View art gallery. I believe that you know what I'm talking about, right Mr. Amoretti?" Detective Doyle continued.

Silvio sat silently again, now swirling his drink and sizing up the two detectives. "Detective Williams, yeah, I know you.

From a few blocks over, right? Big swimming star if I recall," Silvio offered up ignoring Detective Doyle's questions, "and now you're back as a detective."

Detective Williams stared back at Silvio, then answered, "Yeah, that's right, back taking down bad guys, although you all seem to be doing a pretty good job of taking each other out for us. Thanks for that."

Silvio's blood boiled at the comment. His face reddened and he gripped the glass so tightly that Detective Doyle thought that it was going to shatter in his hand. "Ok, let's just all keep calm here. We're just trying to figure out what happened," Detective Doyle interjected, trying to keep the situation under control.

"I already talked to the police. I got nothing more to say," Silvio growled, while keeping his eyes locked on Detective Williams.

"I realize that," Detective Doyle continued, "but, see, some new information has come to light."

"And what information would that be?" Silvo asked, slowly turning his gaze away from Detective Williams to Detective Doyle.

"It seems that some of your guys that were at the job are unaccounted for. We're just trying to understand why," Detective Doyle replied.

"You mean Louie? Yeah, we are aware. The situation is being handled," Silvio bluffed, having no knowledge of Louie's whereabouts.

"Ok, and what about the kid?" Detective Doyle continued.

"What kid?" Silvio asked.

"The red haired kid. The one that set up the security system," Detective Doyle replied.

"I don't know about any kid," Silvio replied.

"We have it on pretty good authority that the red haired kid was there," Detective Williams interjected.

Silvio glared at the detective, "You talking to me? You come into my place, say what you said about my associates, and then have the balls to talk to me again?! You better watch yourself, Detective, lots of accidents have happened to wise-ass detectives in this neighborhood over the years."

"It's not the same neighborhood anymore, and you know it," Detective Williams snapped back a reply.

"So angry, detective, it's almost like you have something personal against this kid. Scorned lover, perhaps?" Silvio asked with a smirk.

Detective William stepped closer to Silvio, then bent and leaned on the table to face the man, "I take all of you old school, washed up, worthless mobsters personally. A bullet from one of your guns killed my sister on a drive-by. She was six years old. Gunned down in cold blood because some fat Italian bullies decided that another fat Italian bully needed to die in as public of a spectacle that they could muster. So, is it personal? You're damn right it is. And I am not one bit sorry that part of your band of thugs shot the others and managed to do it without killing any civilians. Perfect poetic justice. I just want to catch the rest of you rats and end all of this once and for all. Now, what about the kid?"

Detective Doyle let out a nearly inaudible, "Whoa."

Silvio stared into the eyes of Detective Williams. While Silvio managed to hold his neutral appearance, inside he felt a mix of emotions. As a younger man he would have tore into Detective Williams, likely choking him with his bare hands. That emotion wasn't the strongest that he felt. He mainly felt an overwhelming sense of sadness. Sadness for the loss of his crew, as well as for Detective Williams and the loss of his sister. He also felt very fatigued. *'Maybe this is it for me. Maybe it is time that I just walk away from this life. Sonny may be right, it's passed me by'*, he thought for a brief second before regaining his composure.

"I told you, I don't know anything about a kid, but if you find him I would love to meet him," Silvio replied, continuing the facade of the heartless mobster. "Now why don't you two get out there and find these guys? Meanwhile, Sonny and I will make sure that our other associates are well organized and ready to help in any way."

"Yeah, let's talk about Sonny," Detective Doyle interjected.

"What about him?" Silvio asked.

"Where is he?" Detective Doyle asked.

"Why?" Silvio asked.

"Because he was there too," Detective Williams replied with his own smirk.

*   *   *

Silvio was crushed. The detectives explained that their source confirmed that Sonny had coordinated the robbery, and was there when they were loading up the vans. Silvios's grandson had gone against his orders and done the heist anyway. His grandson told him to his face that he didn't know anything about any of it. His grandson had lied to him.

'I can't believe that he betrayed me like that. The other guys hurt, but Sonny...', he thought as he clutched his coat tightly at his chest, less to protect himself from the chill in the air but more to subconsciously protect the pain he felt inside.

After the detectives had gone, Silvio also left and started his walk to Sunday dinner at his daughter's house as he had done so many times before. There would be one less attendee at dinner that evening. Sonny had disappeared. Silvio had tried to call him but there was no answer. Sonny hadn't told Silvio that he was leaving, and with no underboss there was no one else for him to tell anyway. Silvio hoped that Sonny's mother would know his location or be in contact with him.

As Silvo walked, he looked up at the sky. It was gray and cloudy, the clouds moving in the wind, changing shape with the breeze. He recalled watching the clouds for hours from the window of his prison cell, looking forward to when he would see them again as a free man. On this day, however, he didn't feel free. He felt old and heartbroken, the years of his chosen occupation had worn him down and practically finished him off in one wretched event.

As he again focused on the sidewalk in front of him he didn't notice the black sedan parallel parked along the sidewalk ahead. As he made his way closer the tinted passenger window lowered. The young Italian pointed the gun at Silvio, who turned with a look of surprise followed by an immediate realization.

"The Commission sends its regards," was the last thing that Silvio heard before the gunshot.

Epilogue

The first newspaper headline read 'ARTFUL DECEPTION' in large block letters across the top of the page. The article included a photo of Dr. Chad Longfellow being escorted by two police officers from the Berkshire College Art School building. His hands were cuffed behind his back. The story, which was originally published in the college newspaper, was so sensational that it was picked up by the Associated Press wire. It seemed like everyone knew about Dr. Longfellow, how he took advantage of one of his 'vulnerable and impressionable' students, and his plan to pull off an art heist in cahoots with the Mafia. Amazingly, Jake, Sarah, and Louie somehow managed to stay out of the story.

"So how long you figure we're going to have to hear about this?" Red asked, lowering the newspaper. He had just finished the latest article which focused on the administrative fallout at the college, including the total restructure of college sponsored art shows. Red was sitting at his stool at the lunch counter of The Blue Heron. It really was his stool, designated with a brass plaque on his place at the counter. This was his only stipulation as part financier of the acquisition of The Blue Heron. His partners were the new owners, Jake and Sarah. They privately returned the bixie to the gallery and received a small reward for their efforts from Jiao Chang, especially after they explained how Jake had gotten involved and what they went through to return it.

The Heron was busy as usual on this Saturday morning. Snow had come making the village sparkle with the feel of a Norman Rockwell painting. Jake and Sarah would set out after the lunch crowd to hike to Jake's pine grove, taking their new golden lab, Lou. Jake looked over at Sarah, catching her eye when she finished laughing with patrons who were enjoying their hot breakfasts on the cold morning. She smiled at him, giving him a little wave before heading back to the kitchen.

Jake pulled on his jacket and stepped outside to put more salt on the front steps. As he pulled his hand out of the bucket of salt, he saw a black SUV with New York plates and blacked out windows crawling towards the restaurant. The SUV pulled to a stop and the passenger window rolled down directly in front of Jake, who straightened quickly.

A blonde woman with a maroon tassel cap stuck her head out the window. "Excuse me, but do you know how to get to Squire Lake Lodge from here? Our GPS seems to be taking us a long way around the lake. "

Jake relaxed and smiled, "Yup, that's right, you have to drive pretty much all of the way around it. But don't let that bother you, take your time and enjoy it. The lake and woods here are truly, truly special."

Acknowledgments

I owe a huge thanks to my family and friends for all their support as I embarked on this adventure. I especially want to thank friends Ron King and Melissa Jankowski for their time and willingness to help make sure I was on the right track; Bryan Lockett for his early inspiration when he wrote his own novels; Bryce Breen for his creativity, motivation, and the countless walks and discussions about our respective projects; my parents Ken & Linda Raymond for creating an engineer that apparently enjoys creative writing; my sister Melissa for her insights and ideas; my amazing boys Derek & Sean and the inspirations that they have become for me; the faculty at The Hartt School of the University of Hartford for their generous assistance; the Schantz Gallery in Stockbridge, Massachusetts, for the early insight into Chihuly glass; The Red Lion Inn in Stockbridge, Massachusetts, where many elements of the novel were first thought through and the first words were typed on the expansive front porch; Artist Isha Nelson for her brilliant pieces; and of course my wife, Jennifer, for her patience and support through the creation of this novel, and the countless times that she listened, read, offered, and counseled.

About The Author

Mark Raymond is a career engineer with a lifelong propensity for storytelling and newfound affinity for writing. He is the father of two amazing sons, and currently lives in Mystic, Connecticut, with his wife and his honeybees. *Beyond The Pines* is his first novel.

Made in the USA
Monee, IL
01 July 2024

61040350R00142